MANHUNT

Dowd picked up the reins. "See if you can track that damn fellow down then, Lane. And of course, be as careful as you can."

Lane sat the bay, watching the surrey out of sight down the ranch road. Dowd had been lucky that Pace had chosen the Short-C for his first killing. Lane didn't have much faith in those two drovers stopping Frank Pace from doing anything he wished to do. A third man riding guard might help. Owen and Evans and the boy would make a fair three-man guard.

Not fair enough in the long run, of course, the long run being about another two days. In that time, were he in Pace's boots, he would have bumped another cattleman for sure, or one or two drovers—or little Matthew Dowd. Broken Iron was the biggest outfit in this county.

Pace would nail Dowd sure as shooting, three-man guard or no. Unless Lane killed him first.

BUCKSKIN #5

GUNSIGHT GAP

ROY LeBeau

LEISURE BOOKS   NEW YORK CITY

A LEISURE BOOK®

September 2003

Published by

Dorchester Publishing Co., Inc.
200 Madison Avenue
New York, NY 10016

ISBN 0-8439-2189-7

Visit us on the web at www.dorchesterpub.com.

ONE

FENTON LANE sat the blocky pinto for a little while, watching the big range cow lunging here and there in a deep sink-hole pit, trying to work herself free. She paid no attention to the week-old calf that staggered behind her, almost belly deep in the black soup. The cow, bellowing in fear, had crapped into the mess.

Lane turned in his saddle, scanning the high meadows for the sign of a single damn drover— just one young Broken Iron buckaroo, anxious to earn his forty dollars a month.

Nothing to be seen but grass, larch trees, and mountains.

Lane muttered in exasperation, reached down to unfasten his rope, fist it, and shake out a stiff, unhandy loop. He spurred the pinto up to the lip of the sink-hole, swung his loop once in an easy circle over his head and threw it. The cow, eyes popping in panic, dipped her head in a lunge, and the loop struck her shoulder and slid off.

"Jesus Christ." Lane hauled the rope-length in, rebuilt his loop and tried again.

This time, he caught a horn, and was tempted to make his haul on that, and if it broke, to hell with her. He sat the pinto, considering it—then sighed, flapped a wave into the riata, and watched it lift the loop off the cow's left horn. By God, managed that, anyway.

Once more, he hauled the rope, built his loop, and threw it. And this time, by something of luck, he made a good two-horn catch, turned the pinto, dallied to his saddle horn and spurred the horse off.

The cow was a big brute, and the pinto, a mighty strong horse, did some heavy grunting as it strained away. Lane was careful to keep his thumb out of the dally—the rope was bar-taut, and creaking.

He turned his head to see the cow scrambling and slipping, down on her knees and up again, slowly making the slope, her neck twisted slightly from the steady saving pull of the rope on her wide horns.

The calf was trying to follow her up, and wasn't making it. It slipped, fell on its side, and slid, calling for Mama all the way to the bottom.

The pinto, still taking the strain, missed a step and seemed near to tripping. Lane yelled a "Hey-hey!", popped in his spurs and the horse farted and took hold, its head down, driving away like a dray horse.

Lane turned again and saw the cow heave up over the sink-hole rim, flanks heaving, her tongue hanging out, foam dripping from her muzzle. The pinto, still taking its last orders, heaved on her once more, so hard that she went to her knees and slid a yard in the deep grass before Lane pulled the cow-horse up.

He stayed in the saddle for a few moments more, waiting to see if the brute was going to come hooking at him, but the cow had had enough. She staggered to her feet, stumbled away from the sink-hole rim, and trotted unsteadily a few yards south before she slowed to a walk, then, still blowing, her hide streaked with sweat and mud, began to graze.

She paid no mind to the calf calling to her from the mud-pit.

Once more, Lane looked around for sight of a cow-poker. Not a damn one of those fools in sight. Every damn one of them off on goose chases for loose stock and ending up, more than likely, up to their belly buttons in some mountain creek, splashing around and japing.

Damned if they were worth forty dollars a month! *Four* dollars a month was more like it!

He cast a careful glance at the cow, but she was drifting away eating grass like it was going out of style. Then Lane swung out of the saddle, gathered up his rope, and walked swiftly to the sink-hole rim. The pinto, ground-tied, farted again and stayed put, cropping some grass of his own.

If there was anything plain, it was that he wasn't going to be able to rope that little fellow, not with it bucketing around down in that soup. Mud, piss, and manure.

But he'd damn sure give it a try.

Lane built a careful loop, and took his time with

the cast. It settled just over the animal, and the little son-of-a-bitch jumped right through it, bawling for Mama as it went.

Bad luck. But it was a good throw anyway. He hauled in the rope, made his loop and tossed it easy, underhand.

Just missed.

Lane tried four more casts. On one, he got the little bastard by a back leg, but it was too damn slick with mud. The loop slid off.

Lane hauled the riata in for a seventh try, started to build his loop again, then suddenly threw the whole mess on the ground.

"God damn you little piss-ant!"

Lane looked around once more, unbuckled his gun-belt, wrapped the leather carefully around the holstered Bisley Colt's, and set it down in the grass. After a moment, he reached down into his right boot, pulled a long-bladed, double-edged Arkansas knife from a sheath there, and put that weapon with the Colt's.

"God damnit!"

Then he walked to the rim of the hole, and started sliding down. The sink-hole was more than a dozen feet deep, and steep sided. The sides were clay mud, still slick from last night's shower.

Lane got only a few feet down, digging in his boot heels as best he could, when he set his left foot on a very poor spot. That foot skidded suddenly, and when Lane, windmilling his arms, tried to recover, he set his other foot on a place just as bad.

He pratfell like Eddie Foy at the Republic

8

Theater in San Francisco, landed on his butt with a thump, and slid, helpless as a pig on ice, all the way to the bottom.

He went in over his head in the soup down there, almost panicked until he was able to thrash around so as to get his feet under him and rear up for a breath of air. Coated with mud. Was bound to be looking like a human turd, he thought.

Lane spit out some mud, and whatever else was in there, turned to look for his hat, and was butted full into by the calf, come roaring to what it believed was its mother.

They went down together.

Lane shoved the kicking, bawling animal aside, and managed to get up on his feet again. When the calf came right back to him, butting and nuzzling at him for some milk, Lane wrestled him around, gathered the calf up—one arm under its butt, the other under its forequarters—and managed to lift it up out of the mud, hugging it to his chest to keep from getting kicked. The calf was heavier than it looked.

Lane waded slowly through the deep mud, doing his best to keep his balance. He doubted he could catch the calf up again, were he to let it loose. At least the animal was quiet now.

Lane slowly marched out of the deepest stuff, dragging his mud-caked legs, his drowned boots, for every step. It was a considerable effort, and it cost him. Lane could hear his heartbeat thudding in his ears. It was very hard to get a good breath . . . . Too damn long since he'd cowboyed, since he'd done any sweat work at all. Too damn long.

He should have left the little son-of-a-bitch to starve.

When he reached the steep slope up out of the sink, Lane knew he couldn't climb it, not carrying the calf. He'd been a damn fool, of course. Should have brought an end of the riata down with him. The pinto might have backed them both out of this damned toilet of a place . . . Reminded him of a friend's death, some time ago.

Died stuck in a place like this . . . Worse.

He set the calf down on the slope, faced it upslope when it tried to turn back to the pit, and began to push the animal ahead of him, up the side of the sink-hole. It was hard to do, because it had to be done crawling on all fours.

Lane tried to stand up once, and came near to slipping, calf and all, back down to the bottom. That taught him his lesson, and it was crawl up all the way after that. The calf kept balking, too, and Lane came near using his head to butt the little bastard along. Had the slope been any steeper, likely he would have done that.

It seemed to have been a week, at least, from the time he'd slid down into the sink till that relieving moment when he was able to give the damned calf one last shove up and over the rim, and onto grass.

Lane dragged himself up and over, grabbing handfuls of grass for the doing, and was glad to lie flat on his face, getting his breath back.

Too old. Too damn old for this kind of thing . . .

He felt better pretty fast, though, and lay there listening to the locusts whirring through the grass stems, thinking about getting up and onto the

10

pinto. Finding a stream—run at the end of that wooded meadow would do—and getting shut of the mud. The mud reminded him of his friend—head down in a shit-hole . . . strangled in it.

He'd feel some better, getting the mud off.

Lane had gotten to his feet, and picked up the holstered Colt's and the sheath knife, when he heard, faintly, odd yelping sounds. Sounded something like coyote pups, and it was coming from the direction of a stand of larches upslope a hundred yards.

He was looking that way, when the horsemen broke cover, and came riding down on him.

Except for one, who was laughing too hard to stay in the saddle, and pulled his horse up, slid to the ground, and stood half doubled over, hanging on to the stirrup leathers as he laughed.

The riders were all laughing, too. Red in the face from it, from holding the laughter in while they watched him down in the sink-hole, wrestling the calf. Probably his ropework had started them off before that.

Even Dowd was smiling. So was Whistler, the thick-bodied bread-pale ex-Mountie, who ordinarily had nothing to talk or smile about.

"An odd business, for a Regulator!" Dowd called. One of the new sorts of cattle kings, a rich Canadian with money to burn. "Didn't know you were such a hand with a rope, Lane!" More laughter.

The crowd of them must have been peeping at him for fifteen minutes or more, enjoying seeing the gunman play the fool trying to cowpoke a calf out of a mud pit. Lane was not as angry as a younger man might have been, being made such sport of. He knew that much of the drovers' laughter—and some of the boss's, too, likely—came from their having been afraid of him, and angry at themselves for being afraid.

Not that he'd bullied anyone, unless it counted as bullying that he'd knocked Jake Gupp cold with a fence board. Gupp was all right—better after that beating—and had at least a little more sense than his brother, Buddy. Together, for working drovers, they had counted as tough, and must have been rubbed the wrong way when Dowd hired him on as regulator.

"Regulator" sounded better than hoodlum, or man-killer.

Lane grinned up at the cowboys circling him. No need to play spoilsport; cowhands like this—foolish boys, most of them, dirt poor and worn to a frazzle—could use a laugh.

"I guess you fellows never saw a pure gold buckaroo in action before." They liked that, leaning back in their saddles as they laughed, recalling this or that to their friends . . . how he'd tried to rope the calf . . . how he'd gone down the hole without a line . . . and how he'd crawled up out, nose to the calf's butt to keep him straight.

"Ole Fen 'nose' what he's a-doin'!" one of those idiot boys called out and they were all off again. It had made this a special day for them. How the tough gunfighter Dowd had brought from Denver turned out to have forgot anything about handling beeves. Too busy, likely, getting in bad card games

12

and shooting real drovers for sport! They were like children, as innocent and as cruel, too, if crossed when they were all together. Their work left them hungry for any kind of pleasure—notably now, the pleasure of ragging the boss's hard-case.

"I'm serious, now," Lane said. "What you boys just saw is the latest word in pure, A-number one cowmanship, as practiced in the great State of Kansas."

The drovers loved that, hating the Kansans, who robbed and jailed them at the end of each long drive to those distant stockyards. The Coloradans called Kansas cattlemen "Loaders," meaning they could only handle cattle to run them up ramps into railroad cars.

"I'm serious, now," Lane said. "Didn't you boys see me catch that calf's right hind with my loop, just to clean the mud off that leg when it came free?" He shook out a loop of his tangled riata, as though to demonstrate, and the young cowpokers made to spur away in mock terror. "Say, listen," he said, "if one of you boys will just hold still . . ." More galloping around, with yells of terror, and "Look out, there, Charley! He's a-goin' to toss that loop right over yore pinkey finger!"

Dowd, probably not caring to see his Broken Iron horseflesh run for nothing, called the funning down. "All right, now! I say that'll do! We've had our fun . . . about time to get back to work." He pronounced 'about' like a Scotchman. "Aboot."

The drovers quieted at once, settled right down, turned their horses and trotted off, paired up, as

Broken Iron liked to have them for rough country work, and only a few of them grinned over their shoulders at Lane, standing, coiling his riata, and covered in mud and manure from head to foot.

"Mister Guthrie has come out with some disturbing news," Dowd said, sitting his handsome bay mare, and looking down at Lane, hunkered down naked in a cold and clean little run called the Little Chicken. Most of the mud was gone; Lane was rinsing the last of it out of his hair. Some of it, smelling of cow crap, had dried and caked there.

"Very disturbing," Dowd said, apparently feeling Lane wasn't paying close enough attention. Whistler, the ex-Mountie, sat his horse next to his boss's, silent as usual. An odd man. Lane had thought him a mute when he'd first met him, but Whistler wasn't mute. He simply hated to talk, and did as little of it as he could. Lane imagined that the Mounties had had to let him go, when the no-talking got to where it hurt his law-dogging.

Dowd seemed to find him a comfort, though. Fellow Canadian. Probably could handle a gun well enough, once he'd gotten it out and cocked. Liable to be a while doing that, from his manner, and the flap holster he wore.

"What news was that?" Lane said. Dowd was as close to a midget as a grown man could be and not be a midget. He didn't enjoy much funning directed his way. Probably scared somebody'd call him Tom Thumb.

"Indians," Dowd said. "Difficult as I find it to believe, in this day and age."

Since the last bad Indian trouble in Colorado had been a good two years past, Lane could understand what he meant. Some Crow had come over from Montana and stolen horses then, and killed some damn fool drunk who'd ridden after them.

That was the Indian trouble.

"Stealing horses?"

"No," Dowd said, and his little pinch-nose spectacles reflected the sun. "They have mutilated Mister Boetha's cattle—twenty head. And they've killed a drover who caught them at it."

Boetha was small beer in the Stockman's Association. Lane had met him at a meeting in Grover, when Dowd took him in to show off his new revolver-hand to his friend. Imported goods, fresh from Denver—and, despite looking a mite trail-worn, and old enough to be past it, come with a startling recommendation from the county sheriff up there, having been caught in a bank robbery and killing three men in the ensuing fight, so sparing the county considerable expense and trouble.

The sheriff, a man named Todd and more of a politician than a lawman, had nevertheless sized up Lane well enough to want him out of Denver and the county. So he had peddled him off to Dowd, as just the hard-case a poor cattleman needed, whose 40,000 acres were being invaded by grasping, greedy, conscienceless sheepmen.

Lane had needed the money, and been wary of

sheriff Todd, who despite his belly and the cast in his eye, was no fool. So he'd signed on for Broken Iron, at two hundred dollars a month (which Dowd counted out to him himself, every first day, and very slowly). It had seemed to Lane that Dowd was beginning to regret the hiring, Parris and his sheep people notwithstanding. This Indian thing looked to be a way to get some work out of his hard-case at last.

"Crows?"

Dowd's spectacles twinkled again. "I have not the least idea." Lane's business; not his. "I simply don't want the savages destroying my animals and killing my men."

Lane thought he had gotten the last of the mud and cowshit out of his hair. The Little Chicken ran down cold. He stood up and climbed out onto the bank, where his still-wet clothes lay stretched on the grass, steaming in the hot afternoon sunlight.

He climbed into his smalls, feeling Dowd's gaze on him. Likely counting the scars. His shirt and trousers felt as wet and cold as the Little Chicken, but he forced them on. Looked like time to earn that fat two hundred dollars a month.

"Akins," Whistler said. His word for the day.

"Yes," Dowd said, "Marshal Akins is pursuing them, Guthrie believed in the direction of the Hills." Grover people called the near cordillera of the Rockies 'The Hills,' probably to make them seem less of an overbearing size.

Made sense. Indians would be fools to double back to the Gap. They'd likely try for the high trail past the shoulder of the Old Man. Old Man was a low mountain, with what some folks claimed was the face of an old man cut by the weather into its north face. Lane had never been able to see it; it just looked like another broken mountainside to him.

But they'd go that way. Were bound to.

And Akins after them.

Strange boy. Had backed Segrue for almost a year, Fort Smith or thereabouts. Which had to mean he was swift with a pistol and guts all the way to back it.

Lane had met him twice—marshal looking a new hard-case over. Akins hadn't seemed very impressed with Lane. No reason he would be. Skinnied-down, trail-worn man in his forties and looking every year of it, grey in his hair, a bad scar down one side of his face. A gunman, no doubt— Akins would have summed him up—a gunman, but probably past it all now. Conning Dowd for board, beans, and two hundred dollars a month. Not bad doin's, Akins must have thought, for an old fart far past it.

And not so very wrong, at that.

Lane had been more impressed with the marshal. Akins was young, even for the killing business, which was a young man's trade more often than not. Twenty-four, no older than that. Said to have put fourteen fighting men under— shot, beat, and jailed a great number more.

The boy was short, bull-shouldered and brown-eyed, looked to have some Mex in him, but apparently did not. He had a bulky, sullen presence to him, very much like a he-cow bothered by flies and the heat. Something that said, 'Leave this one alone.'

Looked very strong. Very strong.

And quick.

He carried one revolver, and no knife that Lane could make out. The revolver was a blocky, fat-barreled British weapon, a double-actioned Wesley, it looked like. As dark, bulky, and dangerous as the boy who carried it.

Carried it in a shoulder holster off his left shoulder, slung low, down along his ribs on the left side.

It looked like a slow draw, try how you would. But it couldn't be, or young Marshal Akins would long ago have been dead meat.

Akins dressed in laborers' clothes, and wore shoes instead of boots. He was clean shaven except for a small mustache, which he kept neat as a lawyer's.

Not impressed with Lane at all.

"You be cautious on how you use that iron," he'd said, resting the weight of his lawman's eye on Lane.

"Always am," Lane had replied, and there it had rested, no more said.

Supposed to be taking no sides in the range scramble between Dowd and his friends and Parris' sheep-herders. Holding to the law, and all things equal. If so, he'd find it hard to do in time. Too much bad temper, and money. Too many passions, and firearms involved.

Not to mention that the marshal's girl was a whore at Mrs. Phelps' house. Not to mention that the girl owned sheep like a man, a flock of two hundred and more.

"Get Mister Lane's horse, Kenneth," Dowd said, and Whistler walked his mount down stream a few yards to the grazing pinto, and bent out of his saddle to gather the hanging reins and lead the horse up.

Lane was dressed now and still cold, weighted with soggy denim and wool.

"I sent the Gupp boys down to Faraway to keep the sheep off it," Dowd said, shifting in his saddle. He was an awkward rider. "Some of those people are supposed to be putting their sheep on there as if it were their land owned . . ."

Lane supposed that would do. The Gupps were up to that, anyway.

"Also," Dowd said, in a casual way, as Whistler lead the pinto up, "Mister Guthrie had some word that that fool Parris had sent for a Texan to come up here to fight for them." He sniffed. "Can you imagine that? Bringing one of those drunken savages up here to shoot people down?" He took out an orange bandana and wiped his nose. A touch of hay fever.

"The fellow's name?"

"Good God—how should I know?" Dowd turned his horse's head and drifted off, Whistler falling in behind him, without a fare-thee-well.

Well, Lane had his marching orders. Get on up to the Old Man, find Akins, and help him kill Indians if he needed help. Anyway, make sure that no Indians circled back onto Broken Iron to kill stock and drovers.

It would all likely be easier than getting that damn cow and calf out of the sink-hole. And it wasn't as if he'd never driven, either. He'd cowboyed in Oklahoma, and in New Mexico, too. But that had been quite a while ago. Never been much of a hand with a rope.

He turned the pinto's stirrup to him, tucked his boot toe in, and swung up into the saddle with a grunt. The horse was still fresh enough for a ride at good pace.

Lane took a sight on the Hills, spurred the pinto lightly, and rode off across the meadow at an easy canter, reaching down to slide the Henry from its saddle scabbard as he rode, half levering the action to check it, and hearing the faint rattle of the .44 shorts in the tube magazine. A nice weapon, if you cared for rifles and got in close. Nothing to a Sharps, of course. Lane had always felt that if you wanted a rifle, it might as well *be* a rifle, and that meant a Sharps.

With the money he was making from Dowd, might be he could pick up a used one. Some woreout buffalo hunter with no more buffalo to hunt, tired of carrying that weight around to show off. Teamstering, now, and down on his luck. Had to be plenty of those fellows around with a fine rifle to sell for cash.

The Henry would have to do for now. Might be handy, if the Indians were in thick cover and determined to be lively. If there were any Indians at all, and the butchering and killings not rustlers' work.

Dowd was paying him to handle it either way, of course.

Whether Akins wanted him along or not.

Whether Akins wanted him along or not.

There was a willow fringed creek ran down the Old Man's shoulder (if you saw an old man up there on the granite face at all) and Lane pulled the pinto up for a breather on a slope above the creek run.

It was a place that some Indian boys might dismount to rest at, even if they thought they might be pursued. Indians had their own ways of doing things. They ran in a different way than whites, as well. Lane had never been in the Indian-fighting set that had clustered 'round the cavalry posts, sucked up to the officers and so forth, to do some scouting jobs that amounted to nothing much. It had been his experience that Indians, ever the fiercest of them, tended to be more peaceable, more *restful*, than whites, barring some wild boys out on a drunk. Red men didn't seem to care for all the niggling trouble that a serious war brought with it. If Custer and the Army hadn't been such damn fools and had just hung back for a while, that whole pack of Sioux and Cheyenne would likely have quarreled, and horse-raced, and dog-stewed for a time, and then drifted on over to Canada without a shot fired.

Were exceptions, of course—or had been a few years ago—Comanche. White Mountain Apache. They'd enjoyed the trouble of wars for a while.

He leaned against the grazing pinto's shoulder,

the brim of his Stetson tilted down against the bright noonday sun. Up here, up in the high country, the mountain sunlight seemed to reflect and flash from the broken stones, glittering with quartz and fool's gold, and from the bright green mountain grasses as well, in constant stirring under the wind.

A shining day. Lane breathed in the sweet, tangled scents of grass and fresh water, the dark smell of the pinto's sweat. A good horse, even if not his own. Broken Iron's. Dowd's. Still a good horse. No speedster and no skirter, either. A solid horse. God knew, better than that damn brown that had shyed at nothing, moving faster than it had in months, and dumped him in a gully with a sprain in his wrist, and the wind knocked out of him. The brown had been more farmer's pig than horse. The old bait gone now, to draw a water cart in Orville, and good riddance. Gone a year, and damn good riddance.

The pinto snorted softly, and Lane raised his head and looked around. Wouldn't be the first fool to daydream his hair right off in Indian country. He reached around the horse's broad chest to slide the Henry up and out of the saddle scabbard— then walked off into a stand of birches, leaving the horse ground-tied.

The birches trailed on down the slope to the creek, and Lane, the light rifle balanced in his hand, walked swiftly down the shady treeline toward the fast water. This high above it, he could hear the water thrashing softly through the rocks below. High, cold mountain water. Too far below, too much of a climb down and then up again to be taking the pinto to water here; he'd drink the horse at Bull Pond, three miles further on.

At a place where a birch had been pulled down and stripped of bark by elk, Lane stopped, sat down, and pulled a small brass-tubed telescope out of the waistband of his pants. It was a little instrument, not much use for real distance, but it tripled the size of things when looked through, and that had been very handy in times past.

He glassed the creek below from falls to final run out of sight, and took his time about it, looking for the smallest smudge of smoke, for pony tracks in the sandy shoals, for broken-branch bushes. He took a good time doing it, and would sometimes swing the little glass back to a place he'd already looked over down there, just to be certain.

Then, when he'd done that, Lane swept the whole creekbed again swiftly, from right to left, from up-slope to down, to be doubly certain.

He saw a movement in the bright unsteady circle of the glass. Stopped and went back to that. A grey horse singlefooting up the further bank, stepping high. The man on him wore a Derby hat, and a short canvas jacket with pockets in it.

Young Marshal Harley Akins, big as life.

He must have spent the morning looking through the breaks on the south slope of the mountain, to be climbing the creek now. Lane had figured him to be well up ahead already.

Lane kept his glass on the horseman for a while longer. It was the first time he'd seen the marshal mounted. You could tell a good deal about a man from the way he rode.

Akins was no pleasure horseman. He rode the big grey the same stolid way Chicago workmen rode their trolley cars to work. He rode in a solid block, like a chunk of wood, and held the grey together with the strength of his hands and arms.

A determined young man and a stiff bender.

Take a great deal of killing, a fellow like that. You were liable to have to use a head shot at the finish, no matter what wounds you'd made before.

Lane watched him for a while, then put the little telescope away, got up from the birch log, and started back up the slope. They would be going the same way. It would be interesting to see how long it took Akins to spot him.

He climbed to the steep meadow where he'd left the pinto, slid the rifle back into its scabbard and mounted. He reined the pinto around, and began to ride along the upper edge of the meadow, staying high above the mountain creek below, screened from it by birch, and alder, and by the narrow lodge-pole pines that grew in stands together where the mountain slopes leveled off.

Lot of birds about, playing in the berry bushes, red and choke-cherry, that grew along the way. Some bears might be feeding in the rough there, with their cubs. Would be wise to keep that in mind.

Lane wondered who the Texas tough was that Parris had hired to come up. Must have paid a pretty penny. Texicans didn't care to travel out of Texas as a rule, unless for work and pay. There were a bunch of Texas gunmen, young and old, some of whom would know Lane by sight. Had sure as hell known Buckskin Frank Leslie, and were unlikely to be put off by grey hairs and a face scar and a changed name.

It would be interesting, if the man proved one of those.

The trail was getting steeper now, heaving up higher and higher toward the shoulder of the mountain. In a while, they'd be at Bull Pond, and the pinto would have his drink, and Lane would get down and put his face into the water and drink with him.

No one carried canteens in this country. Water was there for all, along every trail below the mountains.

And past Bull Pond, he'd pick up Akins' track again, cross the creek high, and find out if the men they were chasing were there at all—and if they were, were in a mood for shooting.

TWO

ONLY THE Kiowa killed like that.

Pace slid out of his saddle, cocked the Spencer, and walked over to look.

God knows he didn't want to. Not that he was worried about the Indians—not too worried, anyway—because by the signs, those artful butchers were long gone. It wasn't the Indians, it was what they'd done he didn't want to see.

But he had no choice.

When a man saw two wagons busted and burned and three dead men stretched out and sliced to pieces and roasted slow, well, a man could still be cautious and ride around. But when a woman hung naked, ripped and dead from a nearby tree, and a little toy hobby-horse lay stomped and broken on the ground, any man who *was* a man would have to stop and go on in. There was always a chance—a slim chance—that the kid had gotten away, or that the Kiowa hadn't killed him. Indians were funny about kids; sometimes they killed them cold; sometimes they took them as slaves; and sometimes, if the kid showed courage, they left them alone.

Not this time.

Pace found him only a few yards from where they'd hanged his mother when they were through with her. He was a little boy, maybe six or seven. They'd cut his throat.

Pace hoped he'd died before he saw what they did to his mother.

The burying took a while. There was no question of Pace not doing it. He had a great respect for death, which was natural, considering that death was his business.

He buried each dead man in a shallow grave, but he buried the woman and child together. It was hot work. A Colorado summer wasn't a Texas summer, but it was warm enough to make a man sweat through his shirt, digging graves.

As he dug, Pace wondered what the Kiowa had been doing raiding so far north and east; they were west Texas Indians, and since the army had pretty much broken them in the seventies, they'd stuck to raiding into Mexico, or hitting an occasional panhandle ranch for beef or some dumb unready cowpoker.

The poor murderous red sons-of-bitches. They'd just about been driven to the wall, run down in their own country like wild turkeys by every blue-belly with a federal commission and a yearning for headlines back east.

And they'd cost him a good part of the day's riding.

He finished the last grave—the woman and her boy—tossed the broken-handled shovel down, and stretched to ease his back from all the digging.

He'd be a day late, getting into Grover. A day

27

late meeting Parris.

He picked up the Spencer from where it leaned against a charred wagon-side, and walked back across the clearing to the tethered dun. The big gelding nickered and bumped him with its nose.

"You don't like that smell, do you, boy?" Smells of burning and death.

Frank Pace had smelled those smells the first time when a Yankee patrol had come through Terhune, Texas, when he was only fifteen.

He'd been up in the pine barrens above the soddy, bringing in the stock, when he'd heard the first shot. And by the time he'd caught up the roan mare, forked her, and galloped on down to the house, it had all been over.

His father, invalided home from Hood's brigade, lay dead out in the yard, his crutch broken under him, his Dragoon Colt still hot from firing clutched in his hand. His brother, Louis, lay further down, by the stream. Dead. Eleven years old.

Later, days later—after the neighbor women had come, and comforted, and stayed a day or two, and gone—Frank's mother had broken her silence to tell him what had happened. How the raiding Union cavalry had come storming down the draw as if they were charging a regiment, had ridden Louis down as he ran to warn his father and had been met by John Pace, leaning on his crutch in the yard, his pistol in his hand.

He had managed to wound one of them before he went down, shot to pieces. And then they were

28

gone. Ashamed maybe, of having killed a child and a cripple, they hadn't stayed to plunder.

Frank's mother told him what had happened. Then she had returned to her silence.

A year later, she was dead.

Pace slid the Spencer into the saddle scabbard, gathered the reins, and swung up onto the dun with a grunt of effort. He was soaked with sweat from all that digging. Been a long time since he had to do chores of any kind. Killing men didn't take all that much time—or effort, either, come to that, unless he had to use his knife.

He spurred the dun lightly, and headed west out of the clearing, back along his original trail, making for the first sawtooth ridges rising high in the distance, and the spine of the Rockies looming up into towering snow-sugared peaks behind them.

This was high country, greener and more broken than the Texas flats, the hillsides rich with pine and larch and mountain villow. And almost every mile, Pace had seen a bright little mountain creek splashing down a green gully or foaming through a willow draw. A lot of water up here. Pace had known good men killed fighting for springs not a tenth as full as any of these mountain brooks.

Rich, green country. And winters probably colder than the North Pole.

He put the dun to a steep meadow bank, and the big horse scrambled up it like a cat. The dun had a nasty temper and it liked to bite but it was a very strong, fast, and staying horse.

But big as the dun was, Pace, in old deep brown woolen trousers, seemed oversized for it, his long, bony legs, hanging down below its barrel, his tall, lanky body towering over the horse's withers as he leaned forward to ease the climb.

When the war had first started, Pace's friends had taken to calling him "Old Abe" after the new Yankee President. And he did look just like him; over six feet tall at fifteen (and bound to reach six and a half feet when he was grown) and bony, awkward-looking and lantern-jawed. "Ugly as sin," his best friend, Ollie Parker, had said.

"Ugly as sin . . ." And he supposed that he still was. A big, tall, ugly, lanky man. For certain sure, no decent girl had ever looked at him twice. Though his mother had said he had real pretty eyes. "Pretty as a girl's," she'd said. Big, soft, black, and sad.

Nobody else had ever said his eyes were pretty, though. None of the thirty-one men he'd killed had thought them very pretty.

Pace reined the dun up at the top of a grassy ridge, and sat relaxed in the saddle, taking a look round the country just in case the Kiowa had doubled back. It would be strange, him and the Kiowas—Texas people—to meet way up here, and go to killing each other just like they were home.

He reached down to ease the big Remington high on his right hip. He'd always favored Remingtons, and the .44 was converted from cap-and-ball to cartridge. A sturdy piece.

On the other side of his gunbelt, a blacksmith-made Bowie rode in a rawhide scabbard. It was a bigger knife than most men carried now, with a foot long blade. But not outsized for a long limbed man, six and a half feet tall.

The sun was setting fast now; he'd lost the afternoon burying those people at the wagons. He would certainly be another day getting into Grover—should make it just before dark tomorrow, if that fellow in Boulder knew what he was talking about. Same man talked a lot about sheep, too, and what a trouble they were to the cowmen in the state.

Well, he was right, and it was trouble that was going to put money into Frank Pace's pockets.

He camped at the head of a narrow draw, under a small stand of green larches. Staked the dun out —the big horse wouldn't abide hobbles—and sliced some bacon for supper. He fried it up in his little tin pan, and crumbled the last of his hardtack biscuits into the bacon grease as the meat cooked.

It was good, but there wasn't much of it.

When he finished, Pace got out his book (he always carried one book of some kind in his saddle bags) lay down close to the small campfire, and read a chapter straight through. He didn't have to follow the words with his finger or move his lips when he read, either. His mother had taught school before she married and she'd taught her own boys thereafter. It was true that Frank wasn't the reader Louis had been but he could still get through a book, and enjoy it, too.

31

This one was *Oliver Twist*, by Charles Dickens. Pace had read it before, once. But it was just as good the second time through. He'd read *David Copperfield*, too, but he hadn't liked that one. There'd been some things in that one that he hadn't understood.

He finished his chapter, and got up and kicked dirt on the fire. He didn't like sleeping with a fire that might bring people in on him when he didn't know it, especially with the Kiowa in the country. Then he rolled himself in his soogins with his head on his saddle, and went to sleep hearing the sound of the night wind combing through the trees.

He dreamed of the fight he'd had with Clay Allison. It had been a quick fight—one shot from each of them, and both of them hit and down on the floor of the old *Seguaro*, in Waco. Pace had shaded Allison on the draw, but not by much—not by enough. Allison had been drunk as usual, just coming on to killing-drunk.

At first, the bystanders had been disappointed. They'd been hanging around the saloon all day, watching Pace and Allison talk and play cards and fool around with the girls. And the word had gone out: Clay Allison and Frank Pace have met at last and they're both at the *Seguaro*, drunk as skunks and ready to fight.

Which they weren't—not ready to fight, anyway. They had gotten along pretty well, considering Allison was a prosperous rancher, and a well dressed ladies' man in a gray suit and vest while Frank had looked his usual scarecrow self, like some homely saddle bum off the prod, and couldn't make any girl without paying her three dollars.

So for a while it seemed there wouldn't be any trouble at all. But Allison kept drinking. And drunk, he turned from a nice-spoken gentlemanly man, to a vile-mouthed mad dog. Pace had never seen a man change so.

And Allison had spoken to Pace, finally, in a way he couldn't bear. And Pace had called him—and they'd fought.

Allison had been wearing a cross-draw, and he'd pulled a parrot-gripped .38 as quick as a wink. He'd drawn it as he was lunging up out of his chair just across the table, and Frank had kicked his own chair back and over and drawn and fired as he went.

He'd hit the floor and rolled free of the chair, knowing that he'd put a .44 slug solid into Clay Allison, deep into the left shoulder. Then he'd turned his head to look along the floor to where Allison must have fallen—and Allison had been stretched out in the spilled beer and scattered cards, grinning at Pace like a devil out of hell.

His gray vest had been wet with blood from that solid hit, but his bright blue eyes had been shining like a child's at Christmas. He'd shot Frank in the guts, laughed at him and fallen back, out cold.

Pace had woken up in Mother Mercy hospital with an old Mex doctor probing for the bullet. He'd been very lucky. The .38 had driven through his gunbelt, and then his belly muscles and had run out of steam before it could bust his guts.

He was out of the hospital in two weeks. Allison,

he'd heard, had had less luck with his wound. It had infected, and nearly killed him.

The people in Waco had been satisfied, though. Two first-class guns had met and fought. The handsome, romantic Mr. Allison, and "that Caliban," as the *Waco Times* called Frank Pace. And both had been suitably shot.

Pace dreamed again that he was lying on the saloon floor. "I've shot him," he was thinking. "I've shot him—and I'm still alive . . ." He turned his head to see. And Clay Allison lay grinning at him, pointing the parrot-gripped .38, his eyes as bright as a happy child's . . .

Pace woke with a grunt and a heave, grabbing for the Remington, then lay still, wide-eyed, staring up at the stars.

The night had gotten cooler; the wind had died down, though, the leaves stirring only softly in the dark.

Pace wiped the sweat off his forehead, turned on his side, and tried to get back to sleep.

Not many fights took him like that so he dreamed of them, years later. Ben Thompson had told him once that he dreamed of his fights all the time and each time was as bad as the fight itself had been. That would be hard to bear.

He woke at dark before dawn with a cock-stand that wouldn't go down, even when he pissed. It had been a long ride from Boulder and the whore he had there hadn't liked him, anyway. Most of them didn't like it when you tried to talk with them.

He wished to God he had some coffee left. He

34

could go without a food breakfast if he had to—
had done it plenty of times. But he missed the
coffee something fierce.

By first light, Pace was up in the ridges, riding
the big dun hard through the willow scrub that
bordered most of the meadows up there. It was
pretty country, sure enough, but tough on a
striding flatland horse just the same. But the dun
wasn't a horse a man could baby, even if he
wanted to. The big gelding would take advantage
of that right away and start balking like a mule. So
Pace spurred him up through the willows, holding
his Stetson brim down to cover his eyes from the
whipping branches as they bucketed through.

It was when they got through the patch that
Pace saw the first of the sheep. He'd seen some
cattle earlier, grazing out across a clearing, but
this was the first bunch—flock—of sheep he'd
seen up here. They were healthy looking animals,
as far as he could tell. He'd never had anything to
do with them, as stock.

He rode on through the flock—they scattered
away from the dun as he went past—and headed
down a long, grassy slope toward a little wooded
valley below. Some sort of bustling grassbirds
rose and flew away as he rode down. And it was
right then, sounding out of the whirring of those
birds' wings, that he heard the shots.

Pace pulled the dun up hard and sat high in the
saddle, his head turned, listening.

The shots came again.

It wasn't the Kiowa. In an Indian fight, you

35

might hear a shot or two, then somebody yelling, or screaming, then another shot or two.

But whoever was firing down in that valley was cracking off round after round; it sounded like a war down there, even though it was only two or three weapons firing. Only white men used up ammunition like that.

Pace had a choice: he could ride all the way back down the mountain, ride south for an hour or two, then cut west again, or he could ride straight across that valley and go on about his business. he was late already, a day late to meet Parris.

He listened to the firing, more sporadic now, and looked to see any of the people down there among that thick stand of live oaks tracing a small stream's path through the valley. He couldn't see a soul; the tree tops formed a thick green cover over whatever the action was down there.

The hell with it. He was late.

Pace set the spurs to the dun and headed down the slope at an easy canter. He started to reach down for the Henry, then changed his mind; with cover so thick down there, any shooting would be pretty close-in work. And up to fifty yards or so, he was better with the Remington than he would be with any rifle.

In a couple of minutes, he had ridden down out of the open meadow and into the trees. It was dark and shady under the canopy of leaves. He drifted the big dun along between the rough-barked oaks, stepping it lightly through the carpet of fallen twigs, tree trash and acorns.

Now only a rifle was firing, up ahead. A light

rifle—a .22, probably. If it wasn't for the other pistol shots and the rhythm of the shooting, it might have been some ranch boy out potting squirrels with that .22.

The firing was louder now. Pace ducked slightly when he heard a round go snapping away into the trees just off to his left. He sure as shit didn't want to be hit by some damn fool's stray shot when he was just passing through.

Then he heard a man shouting—sounded mad as hell—and just after that, a volley of pistol shots. The noise was off to his left—probably some kind of clearing there.

Pace had just neck-reined the dun to the right, to angle past all the commotion and go on his way through the woods, when he heard a woman screaming.

He pulled up and listened.

She wasn't shrieking in pain or terror. She was screaming with rage. He couldn't make out the words, but she sounded mad as hell.

Ordinarily, Pace would have kicked up his horse and gone on his way and to hell with other people's troubles, woman or no woman. No woman had ever brought him anything but trouble, that was for sure. And no man ever lived longer by minding other people's business. That was for sure, too.

There were two more shots from the .22, the sound oddly muffled by the thick woods, and a man's voice yelling.

Pace turned the dun toward the sound of the shooting before he'd even decided to do it.

37

You damn fool, he thought. Here you go about to make a prime jackass out of yourself.

But he knew why he was doing it. It was that lady the Kiowa had killed. That had upset him, and there was no use thinking that it hadn't. One woman murdered in this country was enough—although from the sound of her voice, this lady might be the one doing the killing.

And he saw he was right, at least so far, when he guided the dun to the edge of a small sunny clearing, damn carefully, and reached out to part of the leafy oak branches blocking his vision.

A man lay dead on the ground. He looked to have been shot in the face. A cowpoker, by the look of him.

Then Pace heard two men start to shout just to the left of him, behind some oak saplings. They were so close their voices had made the dun start and shift nervously.

"Oh, you dirty cunt, you!" one of the men yelled.

"Jake, come on—it's no good . . ."

"Get your fucking hand off me—I'm going to kill the bitch! It's my brother out there dead, isn't it?"

The other muttered something Pace couldn't hear.

"Come on, then!" the first man said. He had a loud voice. "Let's finish it!"

Pace heard some brush crash and a man come riding out into the clearing. And a moment later, another man rode out after him.

Pace figured the first man was the one with the loud voice. He was a cowboy, too, mounted on a nice bay Morgan colt, a real good horse for a plain cowboy to be forking. He was a stocky looking man, with a round red face and a buckskin hat with its brim turned up in front.

"Dammit, think again, will you, Jake?" the man behind him said. He was a fat man, a cowboy, too, riding a bony gray.

"I *have* thought—now come on with me, you yellow dog!" And he cocked his pistol, a long-barreled Peacemaker.

Just then, Pace saw something move across the clearing over past where the dead man was lying. He had to push a branch aside to see what it was.

It was a woman in a calico skirt and her brown hair done up in pigtails. She was standing up behind a log yelling something at the two cowboys.

No sooner did she do that than the stocky rider with the turned up hat brim threw two shots at her as quick as he could thumb them off.

It was a fair distance for pistol shooting, but he must have come close, maybe even hit her, because she dropped out of sight like a jack-in-the-box.

The stocky cowboy let out a yell at that, and kicked his Morgan into a slow canter out across the clearing, his pistol raised for another shot.

Pace spurred the dun out of the woods at a run.

He galloped past the fat man on the gray who stared, his mouth open in astonishment as Pace went by, and leaned over the dun's neck to call out to the round-faced gunman.

"Hold it, Mister . . . hold your horse up right now!"

The cowboy turned at the shout and the sound of hooves, and took Pace in with one quick look. Then, without hesitating an instant, he spun his Morgan around and drove at Pace, the Peacemaker outstretched, and fired twice as he came.

The first round snatched Pace's hat off his head, the first time that had ever happened to him in a fight. And Pace didn't wait for the second. As it came, he was already swinging sideways to the right, down almost out of the saddle, and he drew and fired one shot at the oncoming rider.

It was a good shot, and it struck the cowboy high in the chest. Pace saw the man's shirt jump where the bullet went in.

But the cowboy had sand. He kept coming, and threw another shot, too. It missed Pace clean. As the cowboy rode past him, the Morgan really sprinting fast, Pace straightened up in the saddle and shot the man in the side.

He heard the thump as the round went in and the cowboy screamed with pain.

Through that noise, Pace heard hoofbeats coming up behind him, and turned in the saddle to see the second man riding up. The fat man had his gun out but didn't look like he'd made up his mind to use it.

But when Pace turned the dun toward him, the fellow raised his revolver, and Pace shot him in the head.

It was a considerable shot, because the fat man was still some thirty or forty feet away. The .44 slug struck him in the forehead and tore it away, so that some of his brains came out and hung over one side of his face like a wet gray dishrag, and fell off in pieces as he shook his head. He was shaking his head as if to shoo away a fly, but it seemed to Pace that he must nearly dead already, injured like that.

As the fat man's horse trotted away at an angle toward the woods, Pace took careful aim at his head again, and fired and missed. Then he fired again, without aiming so much, and hit the man at the back of his head and killed him cold.

When he looked around, Pace saw that the first cowboy, the round-faced man, had ridden off out of the clearing, and he turned the dun back that way and spurred it hard. The big gelding galloped across the clearing, and lunged on into the woods without a check.

Pace found the cowboy not fifty yards away.

He was kneeling alongside a big-trunked oak tree; his shirt and pants were soaked with blood. The blood looked black in the shadow of the woods.

"Oh, you come to look at me, have you?" the cowboy said in his loud voice. To hear his voice, you wouldn't have thought he was hurt at all. "Well, you killed me, you son-of-a-bitch!" He suddenly sank down so that he was sitting with his legs bent under him. He had small dark brown eyes.

"If I had my pistol, you son-of-a-bitch . . . I'd put one into you, right now . . ."

Pace saw that the cowboy still held his Peacemaker in his left hand, but didn't know it anymore. When he saw that the man was that far

41

gone, Pace holstered his gun.

"If I had . . . " the round-faced cowboy said, and he blew a bubble of blood. ". . . If I had . . ." He squeezed his eyes shut as if even the dim forest light was hurting them, and he fell over onto his face and died.

When Pace rode back into the clearing through the vanishing haze of gunsmoke, the woman stood up from behind her log barricade. She had the .22 rifle in her hand.

Pace rode over toward her, and, as he passed, looked down at the dead man he'd seen lying there before he'd butted into the fight. The man, who was a cowboy like the other two, had been shot in the face with the woman's .22.

When he pulled the dun up in front of her, the woman flinched back a little, and Pace could see her knuckles whiten where she gripped her rifle.

It appeared she didn't like his looks. Well, most women didn't.

"Who the hell are you?" She spoke up just like that—still a little scared, though.

She was a good looking woman, Pace thought— girl, rather. Kind of short, and tough looking, with hard blue eyes and dark brown hair done up in those pigtails. Some rancher's daughter, maybe. She had cheekbones on her like an Indian's—probably some Indian blood there, back a ways.

"My name's Pace," Frank said, swinging down from the dun. It didn't seem to mean anything to her. "Sorry to butt in on your party, but you looked like you could use the help."

She flushed at that, and remembered her

42

manners. "Well—you did help. And . . . and I want to thank you, for what you did." She seemed to hesitate. "Is . . . is Jake dead?"

She must mean the loud voiced cowboy.

"He's dead."

"Well, I'm glad!" Her voice was shaking; the shock of all that killing was coming on her. "He tried to kill me!"

"That he did," Pace said, hoping to calm her down. "I don't want to appear curious, Ma'am, but since I got mixed up in this . . ."

"I shot Buddy . . ." she said, staring down at the .22 in her hand. Her face wrinkled up as if she was going to cry, and Pace wished to God he'd turned back up that hill and ridden the other way.

"I don't want to appear . . ." he started again.

"The sheep!" she said, her face red and tears in her eyes. "It was all just because of the sheep!"

Sad as it was to see the girl so upset, Pace couldn't help but think it funny. He'd started on his job already, it seemed. And by ordinary accident.

Parris should be pleased.

"They . . . they work for Broken Iron . . . and Mathew Dowd doesn't want sheep . . ." It was as far as she could get.

Pace stood there, shifting awkwardly while she was turned from him, clutching at a sapling trunk and vomiting hard. He didn't know if he should go and try to help her, hold her head or something. He felt like doing it, but he didn't. It was the damnedest thing.

It took a while for her to come out of it. Pace

43

supposed that decent women were like that, hit hard by killings that way. But finally, she got herself straightened out, and wiped her mouth and stopped sniffling. She gave him an angry look, too, as if it all might be his fault.

"Well . . . I'm all right," she said. "So you can go on your way, now, Mr. . . . . Mr. Pace."

"What about them?" Pace asked, motioning with his head toward the two dead men lying in the clearing behind them. "Miss . . . . ?"

She avoided looking over at the dead men. "My name's Porter. Marcia Porter. I . . . I'll have the marshal send somebody out."

"Out from where?"

"Grover," she said. "Marshal Akins will take care of it." She hesitated, then reached out to shake his hand. "And I do thank you for . . . what you did." Her hand felt very small and warm. But it was a strong little hand.

Marshal Akins, she'd said.

"That marshal—did you say 'Akins?' "

"Yes."

One of the things Pace particularly disliked about his work was surprises. There was little excuse for them.

Martin Parris had written him that Grover had a new marshal from Kansas, brought in since the sheep trouble began. "Some kid," he'd written. And that was all.

"Some kid." If it was Harley Akins—and Pace was damned sure that it was Harley Akins—then he'd just gotten a real bad surprise. Akins had been Pat Segrue's top deputy at Fort Smith. A young boy, Pace had heard, who fancied a shoulder holster, and was quick as a cat on the draw.

It wasn't that Pace was afraid the boy might be better with a gun—that wasn't likely—but he'd be fast for sure, and worse, he'd be willing. Pat Segrue's backup gun would have had to be willing.

Bad news. And news that this Parris had skimped on, when he wrote for Frank Pace. It was a mark against Parris, and Pace chalked it up.

Thinking about that, Pace turned and went to his horse, mounted, and settled himself in the saddle.

"I tell you what," he said to the girl. "Why don't I let the marshal know what happened out here. That way, you can be shut of the business."

"I don't know," she said, looking up at him. She still hadn't moved from behind that fallen log. Pace thought it must make her feel safer to stand back there.

"Is your horse still around here, or do you want me to catch up one of theirs?"

"No," she said, and started to glance out into the clearing, but her gaze flinched away when she remembered the dead men out there. "No, I've got Tiny." She motioned behind her with her head. "He's tied back there."

"Okay," Pace said. And he reached up to touch his hat brim. She sure did look small, standing there.

"You sure you don't want to ride with me into

town, Ma'am?" She shook her head. "Could be more of those cowboys around, and there's Kiowa raidin', too."

"No, thank you, Mr. Pace. I . . . I have to be going on to my place; my stock needs looking after."

Pace had seen she had no wedding ring on her finger, and he thought of asking her why she didn't let her daddy or her brothers look after those sheep for her, seeing all that had happened, but then it occurred to him that she might be an orphan and alone in the world. And if that was so, the question would just make her sadder.

"All right, then," and, as he turned the dun's head, "do you know the closest way into town, Ma'am?"

"Straight up out of this valley," she said. "And over the hill into Gunsight Gap. You'll know it— it's real narrow, like the back sight of a rifle."

That reminded her, and she glanced down at the .22, and then out at the dead men in the clearing. This time she didn't flinch.

THREE

THE GIRL, Marcia Porter, stayed on Pace's mind all the way across the valley and up the steep hill beyond. The dun was still hot from all that dashing and shooting around the clearing. Pace didn't have to tell himself he'd acted the fool down there. Putting his stick in where he wasn't getting paid to put it in was the act of a fool, not a man grown.

Still it had worked out well enough. He had never had the chance before to play the knight in rescue of a fair lady, like one of Walter Scott's heroes. And why not? A man couldn't always be thinking of money, and killing people for money.

Then, just over the rise of the hill, as the dun was snuffling and high-stepping through some choke cherry scrub, Pace saw the Gap. The girl was right as to why they'd called it Gunsight. It was a narrow, towering break in a long green ridge before him. Pace wondered if those Kiowa had come upon this narrow break in the hills. If they had, it would have been a sore temptation to them to set up for business in those close overhanging cliff sides. That pass was made to order for a bushwhacking.

Pace pulled the dun to a halt on the slope of the hill, well back from the entrance to the Gap. He reached back to slide the Spencer up and out of the scabbard, and sat at ease in the saddle, looking the place over. The entrance was a jumbled heap of boulders, fallen from the cliffs above, and there were juniper and pinon pine clinging to the sheer rock faces rising a couple of hundred feet on either side. The passage between those immense rock walls was only about a hundred yards wide. A damned rough and stony hundred yards, too, Pace noticed. Hard ground for a wagon. Tough ground for the dun, for that matter, if he should have to gallop him because of some trouble.

Pace was of a mind to forget the damn Gap, and pull back and ride around it. It was a bad piece of country.

He put away his rifle, turned the dun and spurred it back up the slope; then he reined it in, and stood in the stirrups to get a better look to the north and south of the pass.

It was no damn good. The high, unbroken green on the main ridge stretched out into the distance on both sides of the gap as far as Pace could see; it would take at least another day to ride around it.

No good. He was late already.

Pace swung off the dun, unslung the canteen from his saddle horn, and poured a little water into the crown of his Stetson. He held the hat up so the dun could nuzzle out a swallow or two, then he loosened the saddle girth, and sat down to roll himself a cigarette.

If there was going to be trouble down there,

Pace intended riding into it with a rested horse.

When he finished the cigarette, and had pissed against a pretty quartz-shining rock, Pace caught up the dun, tightened the girth, and climbed aboard. He took out his Spencer again, and spurred the dun into a steady trot, heading straight down the hill for the great jagged doorway to Gunsight Gap.

Echoes was the first thing he noticed in there. The dun's hoofbeats clattered and echoed and re-echoed from the granite walls rising to either side. It sounded as if a troop of cavalry were riding through.

Pace rode light in the saddle, keeping the big dun to that steady trot. The Spencer rested across the saddle bow, Pace's thumb on the rifle's hammer. The dun was smart, as horses go; Pace didn't have to guide him around the fallen rocks and boulders strewn on the Pass's stony floor. He could keep his eyes up, running them over the ledges, crevices, and shadowed shelves that scarred the huge stone wawlls from base to crest. Pace wished that those damn Kiowas had stayed in Texas.

Then, after almost half an hour, he saw the far end of the Gap. There'd been no trouble, no other travelers, nothing living except a pair of turkey buzzards wheeling high over the walls of the pass.

Pace didn't spur the dun for that last stretch out into open country; he held the horse to the same steady gait, and he kept his eyes on the cliff walls. Pace had learned not to get careless when things started to look better.

But no trouble. No trouble all the way through.

The gigantic arching gate of the pass looked out over a long, broad valley, as green and sweet as a land in a dream. A case, for sure, of looks being deceiving or Pace wouldn't have been sent for. Still, it was pretty country. Even prettier than Kerr County, and that was the prettiest county in Texas.

There was a long stand of tall beeches running down along the meadows to the valley below; Pace guided the dun away from them, even though their shade would have been welcome after the stove-dry heat of the Gap. He reined the dun out into the broad meadows, and then relaxed and let the big horse amble.

The meadows were high in summer flowers: bluebells, Queen Ann's lace, and bachelor buttons. Pace remembered going out with Louis to get these kinds of flowers for their mother to put on the table at suppertime, to make some brightness in that dark little soddy. Pretty flowers, but they didn't last. By morning, they'd all be withered and dead.

There was a lesson I might have taken about life, Pace thought. And if I had, I wouldn't have been so surprised about all that's come after.

The sheep must all be in the higher country beyond the valley. Pace saw nothing but cattle in these pastures as he rode. Some longhorn, but mostly that new short-horn stock brought over from England. No saying they didn't grow a fine, tender steak, because they did, but Pace knew men in Texas who swore the short-horns would never take hold. Couldn't stand the bugs, couldn't stand the heat. That's what they said.

And most of these cattle were branded with what looked like a piece of metal broken in two places. Broken Iron. That was the ranch the Porter girl had said those cowboys worked for.

Pace supposed he'd hear about that shooting from whoever ran the ranch. Cattlemen weren't partial to having their hands shot up, even if they'd needed getting shot up pretty bad.

He wondered why those cowboys had felt so free to go firing at a woman the way they had. In Texas, a man who went shooting at a decent woman was liable to get pitched into a bonfire tied hand and foot, however tough a man he might be. It would be strange if Colorado was any different about something like that.

Of course, the sheep and cattle quarrel was a fierce one up here, and good business for him that it was. And even that was a foolish thing, from what George Parker had told him in Dallas. Seemed a Scotchman, who should know, had told Parker that sheep and cattle ran the same range in Scotland without hurting the pasture at all, if they were tended properly.

Well, Pace's money came mostly from people's foolishness, or greed, or spite and old grudges, so it would be foolish of him to argue against any nonsense people had in their minds. It would just cost him money, in the end.

And there was no doubt those boys were only cowpokers. They were nothing like professional guns, though they had sand enough, at least the

51

round-faced one, Jake, had had plenty.

The stand of beeches had petered out over to the left a half-mile, and Pace could now see the trace of a road over there. He turned the dun's head, and spurred the big gelding into a canter. A road over there had to lead right into Grover, and Pace wanted to reach the town early.

He had that kid marshal to see now, as well as Parris.

Grover was a surprise.

It was bigger than Pace had expected, for one thing. And they had a lot of action going; the graveled streets were full of people, even in the heat of the afternoon, and some of them looked like sporting people: gamblers and pimps, other people in the "life."

Pace had heard that Colorado was booming, particularly the ranching, with foreigners coming in with new money to invest, and now he saw it was true. It looked like Grover was a solid little beef boomtown. No wonder the big ranchers were pressing the sheepmen to stay off the range.

No wonder, either, that the townspeople had brought in a fast gun like Akins for their marshal. Most of the men Pace saw in the streets were ranchers and cowboys in for supplies, shop-keepers and clerks, and a few farmers lumbering around on their clumsy wagons stacked high with green garden goods and some early feed-corn, but there were plenty of the other kind, too. Pale men in long coats and fancy linen shirts, with silk waistcoats to hang their watch chains across, and pistol butts poking their coat skirts up at their hips.

A little boomtown for sure. And all the better for Frank Pace. It would mean that the young marshal would have a lot on his mind.

Pace singlestepped the dun along in the traffic, watching out that some farmer or ranch teamster didn't cripple the gelding with a wheel hub. Put a man on a big four-horse dray with a bull whip in his hand, and he seemed to think that it made him a bigger man.

There was such a confusion of signs and billboards hanging off the false fronts of Grover's main street that Pace finally had to lean over to ask some kid ducking across the road where the marshal's office was. The boy pointed off toward the south end of the street, and then ran on his way before Pace could get more definite directions from him.

Pace finally found the law office about where the boy had pointed, roosting between a blacksmith's and a dry goods store. The dry goods looked pretty well stocked; there was plenty that Pace needed after the long trail from Boulder, and the longer, tougher trail up from Texas.

Parris owed him one hundred dollars for a start, just for coming up here to listen to the proposition. Pace had learned a long time ago that people who set out to hire him often changed their minds when, you might say, the whole matter became actual.

There was a deputy sitting out on a cane bottomed chair in front of the narrow jail build-

53

ing, smoking a corncob pipe. He was a hard looking customer with a short beard like a farmer's, and a pot belly that looked to be mostly muscle. A likely man in a bar-room fight, Pace thought. Nothing much with a gun, though. The deputy wore a Colt .45 Peacemaker with a chipped grip up high on his right side, up against his belly.

Slow, Pace thought. It was good to know. A fast deputy could make even a top gun lawman more dangerous. As Akins probably had made Pat Segrue more dangerous.

"The marshal in there?"

The deputy gave Pace a long, slow, considering look.

"Nope."

"He going to be back soon?"

"Maybe . . ."

Pace nodded to the man, turned the dun, and headed back up the street. He remembered seeing a livery sign on a southeast corner a block back. The talk with the marshal would have to wait. Too bad—it would've been better to be first to him with the news.

Pace had had to kill a marshal before. He hoped he wouldn't have to do this one. It made things tougher all around, and would certainly mean that he'd have to leave the state.

Even now, he had to stay clear of Arizona or pass through it damn shadowy.

The livery man was like most of them that Pace had met, a talkative man, always minding other people's business. And a busted-up man, too,

54

limping around tending to the dun, his legs broken more than once by horse kicks from wrestling strange animals in and out of stalls.

"Oh, yes," he said to Pace, hauling a bucket of water in from the pump out back of the corral. "Oh, hell yes, we've got a fine hotel in Grover. Well, we have to, the damn town's bustin' its buttons these days."

"Grover House?"

"That's it, that's the one. Best little hotel in Colorado, too."

Pace gave the liveryman three dollars for a week's feed and keep for the dun, left his saddle to be soaped and oiled—two bits—and carried his saddle bags and scabbarded rifle out behind the livery, down an alley the ostler had pointed out to him, and across a narrow side street to the Grover House. For such a small town, Grover had a damned lot of side streets and alleys. Most cow-towns made do with just one street and a sur-rounding crowd of shacks.

The Grover House was an elegant looking two-storey wood false front painted bright yellow. There was a row of rocking chairs set out on the broad, low porch and, it being two o'clock and just after dinner time, each rocker was filled with a fat-bellied drummer or cattle buyer, come to town to pick up a share of Grover's beef money. Or sheep money, come to that.

The hotel clerk was a tall, thin man, with a bartender's handlebar mustache, and black hair slicked down and neatly parted in the middle. He gave Pace a very dubious look when the Texan came hulking up to the desk in all his dust and sweat.

"I'm sorry, sir, but we're plain full up at the moment. I'd suggest Mrs . . ."

"My name's Pace."

The clerk paused and pursed his lips. ". . . Pace."

"That's right."

"Oh, yes . . . Mr. Pace," the clerk said, riffling through the pages of his register. "Here we are . . . Mr. Parris made this reservation for you for yesterday." He gave Pace an accusing glance. "But we still kept it open at Mr. Parris' request . . ."

He pushed the book over to Pace, who signed it with the scratchy desk pen. Then the man turned to the key rack, took one down, and pulled a note from a mail slot beside it.

"Mr. Parris left this for you." He gave the bell a sharp tap with his fingers, and an old black man in a worn black suit stepped up to the desk and took Pace's saddle bags. "Two-two-three, Bobby."

Bobby ducked his gray head in agreement, and headed off up the hotel's broad staircase, with Pace behind him reading Parris' note as he went.

Mr. Pace: I assume you have been delayed on the trail. I regret that I could not wait in town for you today, but you may rest assured that I will be at the hotel again by dinner time tomorrow, when I shall have the pleasure of making your acquaintance.

Your Obt. Svt.
James McGuire Parris

Fair enough. Pace was just as glad to have the rest of the day to himself. It would be good to get rid of the trail dirt and the trail lonesomes before getting down to business.

The room was on the second floor back, overlooking the alley leading to the livery. A useful location. It was a small room, but clean and new whitewashed, and the bed linen smelled of soap. No question, the Grover House was a classy roost.

Pace gave the old black man four bits, considerably more than he was used to.

"I'd like you to do something for me, dad," Pace said.

"Yes, sir?"

"I'd like you to go pick me up some things at the dry goods. I'll write out a list for you here, if you got a pencil."

Bobby produced a small well-chewed pencil stub and a cigarette paper, and Pace scribbled out his list: from calico shirt to wool pants (sizes stated) to tobacco; lucifers; two boxes of .44-40's; one bandanna; one pair under drawers, large; one can gun oil, small; and one whetstone. He had to use both sides of the cigarette paper.

Pace gave the old man a twenty dollar gold piece.

"And I'll want a bath, Bobby—and the direction of a good dinner, and some fine sporting ladies, too."

"The bathhouse is right out back, sir; they got hot water cookin' out there all the time. And this here hotel's got the best food in Grover, that's for sure."

"And the ladies?" asked Pace, looking through his saddle bags for his piece of soap. "Any place open this early?"

The old man considered the question.

"Well, sir, I understand the ladies over at the Palace are very nice. They are dance hall ladies, there, sir . . ."

"The finest, Bobby?"

The old man considered again, eyeing Pace dubiously.

"Well, sir . . . many of the gentlemen in town . . . well, I understand they visit over to Mrs. Phelps."

When Pace came back upstairs, after a very long, hot bath, and a quick hair trim by the Chinaman running the place, he found old Bobby waiting patiently at his room door with an armload of goods. The calico shirt was colored green and yellow, not the colors that Pace would have chosen, but by and large it was a good shop; everything was there, and Bobby had brought back three dollars change. Pace took two dollars back, received the directions to Mrs. Phelps' house of joy, and then changed into his new clothes and went down to dinner, prepared to eat a steer from nose to tail.

The food was every bit as good as the old man had said it was. Pace had two pan-broiled steaks, potatoes, hot cornbread, a pot of coffee, and two pieces of peach pie. It was a very satisfactory occasion.

When he was finished, Pace strolled out onto the porch, rolled a cigarette, and stood smoking for a while, looking over the traffic on the street. A busy little town. Wagons and buckboards. Some drunk cowpokers went stumbling by, arm in arm, singing *The Bonny Blue Flag*.

Pace finished the cigarette, and strolled down the porch steps, into the bright sunshine.

Mrs. Phelps' looked like a private house, a big, rambling place, painted white with black shutters. The house stood off at the end of a side street, and had a little yard around it, and a fence with rambler roses growing along it. Pace could smell them as he went up the walk.

The place was very quiet. Pace wondered if they were open for business at all. Came over here too damn early . . .

He rapped the door knocker, and had to stand waiting for a while until a small, fat, freckled woman came and opened it. For a moment she was such a respectable-looking lady, all black bombazine and starch, and wearing spectacles, too, Pace thought he must have got the wrong house. But then he heard a piano tinkling away behind her down the hall. Somebody was playing *Step Up, My Ladies*, and mighty lively.

"Yes?" the lady said, not much taken with Pace's looks or the green and yellow calico shirt, either.

"Mrs. Phelps?"

She just stood there, giving him the fish-eye.

"Mr. Parris suggested that I come 'round . . ."

She looked as though that was funny. "James Parris?"

"That's right."

"What's *your* name, Mister?"

"Frank Pace."

She paled as if he'd slapped her. *"Pace?"*

"That's right." He might have known a round-down madam, even in Colorado, would have heard of him. And that was all right. Pace never tried to hide what he was.

Mrs. Phelps backed into her hallway, welcoming him in, and she held out a fat, strong little hand for him to shake.

"I believe we have friends in common, Mr. Pace. I have many old friends in Texas."

Pace didn't doubt it for a minute.

Still chattering away, Mrs. Phelps led Pace down the long hallway. "It's a little early for us here, at least for a weekday, Mr. Pace, and the ladies—well, some girls these days have no sense of responsibility at all. They'll come to work late, or not at all, and think nothing of it . . ."

Then they were in the parlor door, the big curtained room beyond bright with lamp light shining through a haze of cigar smoke. An old man was at the piano in the far corner, strumming away in fine style, and three or four men, substantial citizens by their well cut suits, were sitting on sofas and easy chairs, talking and laughing with the girls. They looked up when Pace came in, stared at his clothes, at the Remington and big Bowie knife, then turned their attention back to the women.

The girls were very nice looking, much nicer than the usual crib meat. Three of them were jolly looking fat young women, two curly haired blondes and a fine, dark, fierce looking brunette. Much nicer than usual.

The fourth girl was something special as well, dressed lke the others only in an open-front red frock and high laced red boots. She was giving Pace a very cold look.

It was the girl from the clearing.

Marcia Porter.

A whore then, and no lady at all.

Pace found himself reddening with embarrassment at the thought of the fool she must think him —to have taken his hat off, and hemmed and hawed at her like a greenhorn.

What had she said? "I have to be going on to my place . . . my stock needs looking after."

Hell, he was looking at her stock right now and it seemed a hairy patch, sure enough. She must have run that horse of hers to get back to Grover to her work by dinner time. Must have left the two cowboys out there to rot.

"That one," he said to Mrs. Phelps. The fat lady hesitated, perhaps because of the look that was passing between them, and Pace said again, "That one."

The other men were watching, too—used, probably, to more punctillio at Mrs. Phelps', some chatting and joking before a man took a whore upstairs.

To hell with them.

Pace took a step and Mrs. Phelps said, "Go with him, Marcia," all in one breath.

A knight to save a fair lady. Pace was tired of the jokes that life seemed to play on him when he gave it any chance at all.

He took the girl by the arm, and gripped her hard as they went to the stairs. Except with her eyes, with that cold and contemptuous look, she made no protest.

As they went up the stairs, Pace noticed she was smaller than he'd remembered from the meadow where the fight was. He had not noticed she had such a round ass on her, and such sturdy legs, with all the hair shaved off to leave them smooth as a child's.

She'd worn no perfume in the meadow. There hadn't been a trace of scent about her there. Now she stank of it.

At the top of the staircase, Pace heard steps coming up behind him. He kept his grip on the girl and turned. It was Mrs. Phelps, tripping up behind them, looking anxious as a hen.

"Mr. Pace . . ." The biddy was breathless from her climb. "Mr. Pace . . ." He stopped to wait for her.

"Marcia . . . please go into your room while I speak to this gentleman."

The girl tried to pull away from Pace, and he held her for a moment, then let her go. She walked across the hall without looking back, opened a door, went in, and closed it behind her.

Pace waited for what the madam had to say.

"Now . . . now," the old lady said. "I don't object —a charming girl . . . a good girl." She peered up at Pace, a fat hen peeping at a possible fox. "Our

Marcia," she said, " . . . a *very* good girl . . . works a business of her own . . . livestock." She put a tiny, fat, freckled hand lightly on Pace's sleeve. " . . . a very, *very* dear friend of our young marshal's."

Pace didn't give a damn if Akin was sweet on the whore.

"She on the trot, or not?"

"Why, yes indeed . . . but, well, kind of a *pearl*, Mister Pace, kind of a *pearl*."

"I won't dust her," Pace said. "Fucking's what I had in mind."

"And straight?" said Mrs. Phelps. "No bumming?"

Pace had had enough.

"You shut your dirty mouth," he said to the old woman, "and get back down those stairs."

Mrs. Phelps peered up at him for a moment more, then seemed to cluck, turned, and went down the stairs at good speed.

Pace didn't fear she'd send the house bully up, or write a note to the marshal, either. She wouldn't want a killing in the house.

He crossed to the door the girl had gone through, tried it and found it unlocked, and went in.

The room was a small, neat, whitewashed whore's chamber, bright enough with the afternoon sunshine falling through a single tall window. There was a white sheeted bed, wide enough for two, with white embroidered pillows on it, and a bedside stand with towels, tin jug and pan.

It was as nice a frigging room as any first class

63

place in Galvestown might boast.

Marcia Porter lay naked on the bed, looking at the ceiling. She looked small and soft, and her body was pale, except for her sun-browned face and forearms. The rest of her skin was a soft, soft white. She taken the combs from her hair (Pace saw them on the bed stand) and her hair was down about her shoulders like a girl's. Dark brown. As dark a brown against her whiteness as the brown of her nipples—the tangled, curling hair between her legs.

The girl looked at him. "Asked about me in town, did you?" she said. "And then came running."

"I didn't ask about you."

"Liar." The girl doubled her legs up, her knees raised, and then let them fall apart so that he could see a little of the color of her slit, buried in that small patch of hair.

"Here's what you want, Sport," she said, not looking at him. "Pull out your package and get to it; I'm not here for company."

Pace felt like the worst damn fool that ever was —taken in by a mud-mouth whore 'till he mooned over her like a lady. And now the split-tail was calling him a liar, saying he'd asked after her, saying he'd chased after her.

"Don't call me a liar."

The girl didn't say anything. She lay there with her legs spread so that everything showed, and didn't care. As if he wasn't there at all.

Pace was angry, and angry at himself because

despite her making a fool of him, he had a bone so hard in his trousers that it hurt him.

"How much?"

"A great big two dollars for you, Sport."

Pace put his hat down on a little chest under the window. Then he unbuckled his gunbelt and went over to the bed to hang it over the end of the headboard.

She didn't turn her head to look at him.

Killed two damn people for this little bitch. And now, being treated like a dog. Worse than a dog . . .

He turned his back and sat on the edge of the bed beside her, and bent to wrestle off his boots. He felt embarrassed about being with her in broad daylight like this. She was so damn uncomfortable . . . Should have waited until night, gone to that saloon . . .

He got his boots off, stood, and shucked down his trousers and long underpants, pulling his socks off with them. He was annoyed to feel relieved he'd taken that bath, got clean clothes on. Duding himself up for a parlor-girl . . .

He started to unbutton his shirt, and she said something to him.

"What?"

"I said, don't bother taking your shirt off, Sport. We're not going to be here that long."

Pace tried to keep hold of himself, and couldn't.

He turned very fast, naked except for the shirt, jerked the long bladed Bowie from its sheath on his gunbelt, and was on her.

A big, bony knee drove the breath out of her, and

65

he gathered her hair up in his left hand, a thick, soft handful, and gripped it hard. His weight was crushing her. She lay still under him, not struggling, not crying out.

Pace brought the Bowie's bright blade over, until it rested in the air just over her face.

"You give me one more bit of sass," he said, "and I'm going to cut some of that pretty off you."

She looked up at him, looking into his eyes.

"If you do," she said, grunting the words out under his weight, "Harley Akins will kill you."

Pace smiled, and very carefully, very lightly, cut her slightly on the cheek.

Then she seemed to understand him—and, for a moment, appeared a much older woman, a tired woman, with her youth all gone.

Pace laid the wide, cool, shining knife blade flat against her other cheek, and held it there, and watched her small chin begin to tremble with tears she only just held back.

He had thought it might give him pleasure to take Marcia Porter down to where she belonged, but it gave him no pleasure at all. He leaned sideways to slide the Bowie back into its sheath on his gunbelt, then settled back onto her, sliding his knee off her stomach so she could breathe. He sat straddling her, looking down into her face. Her eyes were closed, her head turned to the side. He could see a tear in the lashes of her eye. The cut was only a line of red—a single shining drop of blood clung to it.

"Look here," Pace said, and hunched forward. His cock, hugely swollen, knotted with veins, swayed before her face. The girl kept her head turned away.

"I said, *look here!*" Pace tightened his grip on her hair, pulling her head up. She glanced at his cock, then up into his face, her blue eyes dull. She didn't look angry. There was no expression on her face at all.

"You'll do it," Pace said, quietly. "You're going to get your two dollars. Now, you give the best Frenching I ever had, understand?"

He took his cock in one hand, and still gripping her hair in his left fist, put the tip of his cock against her mouth, slowly stroking it along her closed lips. The swollen purple head of it left a wet track on her pale lower lip.

Pace shook her head slightly in his grip.

"Do it. It's what I'm paying for." He forced the thing harder against her mouth, forcing it between her lips.

Slowly . . . slowly, the girl's mouth seemed to soften under that pressure, that insistent prodding. Very slowly, while she stared up at him with that odd, dull look on her face, as if he, huge, dangerous, demanding, weren't there at all.

"*Do it!*"

Marcia Porter opened her mouth wide, stretched it wide open, as a woman might who was screaming for her life . . . opened her mouth wide and moaned, snorting for breath through distended nostrils, as Pace slowly forced the massive head of his cock into her—the head of it, and inches of the thick vein-corded root.

It shoved her cheeks out of shape, pushed her

67

head back against the grip of his left fist. Pace saw the delicate muscles in her throat flutter as she fought to accept it, to take the bulk of it into her mouth without gagging.

The girl's mouth was wet and hot around him. Pace felt her tongue working, moving along the bottom of the shaft. She tugged one of her arms free from under his pinning knee, and put a hand on his naked belly, trying to push him away, to keep him from pressing at her so hard. Her face was distorted from the effort to accomodate him, to breathe with the choking oak-hard organ filling her mouth.

Pace pushed her hand away, and rested, straddling her, not moving until he felt her wet mouth ease around him, relaxing just enough so that he could slide his cock slightly back and forth.

He looked down at her and saw that she was weeping. The pain, the fullness, perhaps the humiliation had made her cry. It felt strange; he felt a kind of sickness in his gut, watching her begin to suck on him, feeling the soft pulling of her mouth, her lips, the slippery tickle of her tongue.

Her head was moving in his fisted grip, gently rocking back and forth, just a little bit back and forth. It occurred to Pace that she was becoming a whore again, giving in to whoring again. He supposed she probably liked playing a decent woman . . .

Thought he'd asked and asked, and tracked her down, glad to find the woman he'd talked to, young lady he'd killed two men for was only a buy-butt. Could pay his money, then, and do what he liked with Marcia Porter and her with nothing to say to it.

Not true. Not all true, anyway. He hadn't hunted her down. That had been happen-chance.

She was making wet sounds with her mouth.

Pace let go of her hair, and sat back a little, just keeping his weight up off her breasts. He could feel the brush of her nipples against his buttocks as she moved underneath him.

Now she was gone far from being any young lady. He had broken her to being a whore again. Her mouth was hot and slippery as any bearded cunt had ever been; her eyes were screwed tight shut, and her head bobbed back and forth as she sucked on him, gulping, tugging, pulling on it, stretching her mouth wide to take all of it she could.

She gasped and let it go suddenly to sway before her, scarlet and swollen. Then she began to kiss it, licking it, nuzzling at it, her mouth, her chin running with saliva, with the clear fluid seeping from him as she sucked. She was moaning as she did it, and weeping.

Pace had never known a woman to do this with such a will—to love it, to need it so. He felt her mouth slowly begin to pull a great pleasure from him; he felt a sweet ache growing and growing at the root of his cock . . . in his stones . . .

He grunted with the feeling, and leaned forward to rest his hands on the headboard of the bed, arching over the girl's laboring head, her quick, avid mouth. Her throat was soaked with sweat, veins and tendons standing out as she sucked and worried at him. She was making wet noises, snorting, breathing heavily through her nose as she Frenched him.

But it wasn't this that he wanted. He wanted to be with her more than this.

His arms were trembling as he braced himself over her. Still, in all the pleasure, through it, he managed to put a hand down to her soft tangled hair, to get hold of her, to make her stop so that they could lie down together, so that he could have her the way he wanted. But when he put his hand down and touched the back of her head, the smooth softness of her hair; when he felt the tender hollow of the back of her neck, where the long tendons worked, then, he couldn't wait.

He felt as though something was being torn away from him, a feeling of pleasure sharp as any pain. A cord of gold was being pulled out of him, up out of his stones, and out through his cock. It burned him with the pleasure of it.

Pace cried out loud—something he never did—and heaved above her and flooded into the girl's mouth. The jissom spurted into her as he gasped for breath, filling her mouth as she kept sucking and pulling at him, gulping it as it flowed into her mouth, dripping from her lips, her chin, to pool in the hollow of her throat.

Gently now, she licked and sucked at him as he grew limp, burrowing her face into him, under him to lick at his balls, cleaning him as a cat does her kitten. She did that for a little while longer, then slowed, and stopped.

70

Then she lay back on the pillow, looking up at him, through him, as if he weren't there at all. As if she were alone, and had been alone, and had dreamed it all.

Pace's hands were shaking as he got up off her, climbed off the bed, and stood up. He felt all tired out. He didn't know what to say to the girl about having cut her like that. There didn't seem to be enough to say about that.

"I'm really sorry," he said, and had to stop and clear his throat. "I'm real sorry . . . I had no business to put that knife to you."

Marcia Porter turned on her side away from him, as if she were going to sleep.

"I only did that—because you seemed to despise me so. I don't let anybody take me in despite."

The girl said nothing to him.

Pace bent to pick up his underpants and trousers from the floor, pulled them on, and then sat on the edge of the bed to put on his boots. He could feel her weight on the bed just behind him. Could hear her breathing. He got his boots on, stood up, tucked in his shirt, and buckled on the gunbelt.

He walked over to the chest under the window, picked up his hat, then dug in his trouser pocket for his money. He peeled off two dollars, and then another dollar and put them on the chest where his hat had been.

He stood in the center of the room for a moment, looking at the girl. She lay on her side, her eyes closed as if she were asleep. She was a small girl, really. Her skin looked very white. He

71

saw that she had small, pretty feet, like a child's.

"I'm not as bad as I seem," he said to her. "I'm real sorry I scared you so . . ."

She made no answer.

"That cut's not bad," he said. "You wash it and leave it alone," he said, "and it won't mark you at all, not the least little bit." He waited, but she didn't say anything.

"I thought you was a lady . . . and I was thinking of you that way . . ." He walked to the door and opened it; then he said, "Don't you send your boyfriend after me. I'd kill him."

Then he went out and shut the door gently behind him, as if he were leaving a sick room.

Mrs. Phelps was waiting at the bottom of the stairs; the other people were gone from the parlor. Pace could hear someone talking in the back—the kitchen, likely.

"Is she all right?"

"As right as any whore will ever be," Pace said. "I nicked her, but it won't show more than a few days."

The fat little madam turned so pale her freckles looked like spots of ink. "Oh, my God!" she said. "Harley Akins will kill you—and kill me, too."

Pace was getting tired of listening to her.

"He won't kill me and not you, either. Tell her to say she got it helping in the kitchen." He turned away from her and walked down the hall toward the front door.

"He won't believe it," she called after him, keeping her voice as soft as she could, so the others wouldn't hear. "He won't believe it!"

Pace was surprised, when he walked out onto the porch outside, how bright and sunny the day remained. It felt to him that he had been in Marcia Porter's room for much more time than that.

He went on down the walk and smelled the fence roses as he went by. The sunlight was softer now, though. The soft gold of late afternoon.

It had been a day full, sure enough. He felt happy and sad at once. Those feelings were so mixed together that he couldn't tell them apart.

He'd see Parris tonight and then get on with business. The girl would be in the same town with him, all the time.

FOUR

THE SHADOWS were lengthening down the mountainside, the sun lower now, just over the peaks of the Rockies. Lane had been waiting on a shelf of granite for some time. Waiting for Akins to show.

Fine, small saplings of box alder edged the sloping granite slab. It overhung the trail—as much of a trail as there was this side of the Old Man—like a painter's hide, where the big cat might wait for elk.

Akins was due. Lane had seen him again just after Bull Pond.

Of course, he didn't have to wait for the marshal. Just a few minutes ago, across a deep draw so crowded with pine that it seemed a rough-grassed meadow to get over, rather than a hundred-foot drop filled from edge to edge with the tops of trees, he'd seen it.

Just over there, and not more than a few minutes ago, Lane had seen the smudge of smoke drifting down into the pines. That was where the Indians were. Indians, because it was the smoke from a very small fire. And, what was more interesting, strange Indians. Flatland Indians, who

74

didn't know that in the high mountains, fire smoke drifted down, not up.

Not Blackfoot, then, or Crow.

Some flatland Indians, a long way from home. Couldn't say how many. Lane had seen no tracks. The Indians had come the long way round—up the south face, and high enough at that that Akins must have missed their track on his swing south.

They'd be resting now, ready in the morning to cross the Old Man's shoulder deep into the Range. There, any number of narrow valleys led south or north.

No catching them, then—if anyone wanted to catch them.

Akins was coming on slow . . . cautious. Maybe too cautious.

If he didn't show soon, Lane would have to decide whether to go across and take those Indians hisself—which didn't, right off, appear to be the wisest thing to do—or just let them go. Climbing down into the arroyo, then climbing out of it, then jumping those Indians . . . Possible now, or pretty soon, while daylight held.

Not such a knacky notion in the dark.

This late in the afternoon, the breeze came cooler down the slopes, but the granite slab held all the previous heat of the day, and Lane, lying back along the rock, enjoyed the steady warmth against him.

It was a shame to bother Indians on a day like this. Purely a matter of money. Bother the Indians, or get the sack from Dowd.

He would have to bother the Indians, then. Gotten used to lazy doings . . .

Lane heard the pinto shift where it grazed up behind the slab outcropping. The soft jingle as its head came up.

Lane was on his feet and down off the rock in a swift silent scramble, got to the horse and clamped his hand over its nose just as it raised its head to whinny. Lane stood quiet, holding the horse and listening.

For a little while he heard nothing. Soft wind . . . two birds quarreling further down the meadow . . . then, very faintly, the soft squeak of saddle leather.

He pulled the Henry from its scabbard, and then stepped carefully back up onto the outcropping. The trail below was partially screened by the alders. It took a few moments for the horseman to ride into view.

Akins, still plodding along in that steady way.

But not quite in the same steady way. Lane stood watching the marshal, watching the way he was sitting his horse. Differently. Akins was easy in the saddle, now. Relaxed. Different from the way he'd ridden before.

Too different.

Tiredness would make a man slouch a bit after long riding. The usual man. But Harley Akins wasn't usual, and he wasn't the type to ease out when he was hunting killers.

Akins was fooling—pretending to be at ease. He knew Lane was watching. Had known, then, for most of the day.

76

Lane jumped down from the rock, grunting as his boots jolted into the meadow turf, and walked out of the cover of the alder saplings, waving the Henry so Akins would see him. No use having the boy ride on into plain sight of those Indians. Akins had caught Lane out in some way—likely that little telescope had glittered in the sunlight, something of that sort—but it was unlikely he'd know the people he was hunting were not more than a distant rifle shot the other side of that draw.

Akins saw him at once and pulled his grey up. He sat the horse, still with that false air of relaxation, and watched as Lane came down the hillside toward him.

"Been doing some lurking, haven't you, Lane?" he said. "You ought to be a mite more careful when you watch a man through glasses. I saw the shine below Bull Pond." He showed no relief at it being Dowd's man who'd been glassing him and not the people he was chasing.

Lane judged himself careless, watching, and the marshal to be just the smallest bit too young for his job, however tough and quick he might be in trouble. An older man would never have told Lane he'd spotted him or how, or allowed that to show in his manner of riding.

Akins was a little young. Young in the mountains, at any rate, however old in town. In a tough town, this boy would likely be in his home pond up to all the rigs.

"Careless," Lane said. "Must be getting old."

Akins sat his horse and looked down at him,

77

saying nothing more. He looked thoughtful.

"There are four or five Indians over across the deep wash," Lane said. "I assume the folks we've come after." He pointed through a stand of alders. "Through there. Maybe a quarter of a mile across and deep as hell's half-acre."

"You know what kind of Indians they are?" Boy was not too young to ask questions when he needed answers.

"Not mountain Indians. They've come a way, whatever they are."

"Indians," Akins said, and shook his head. He climbed off the grey. "You camping up there?" He nodded up at the granite shelf. "We'll leave the horses there, then, and go across after those red niggers. See if we can settle them before dark." He started striding off up the slope. "After I take a shit," he added.

No objection to Lane's being up here, then, or going along for the fight, either. Akins might feel more comfortable with an older man along, particularly out here in the wild. Came from working with Segrue, likely. It would be interesting to see if Akins leaned on him when the shooting started . . . that is, if they did ever get across that canyon before dark. It looked to be a hell of a hike.

It was every bit as bad as he'd feared.

They'd taken both horses up higher into the trees and tied them there, chewed on a couple of sticks of jerky Akins had brought, and set out, keeping to the alders all the way to the canyon edge.

It was a steep way down, a sloping wall of cracked rock and twisted dwarf pine. These pines, growing from splits and spalls in the stone, were the only handles Lane and Akins had as they climbed down out of the soft late afternoon light, down into a pine-green evening, that grew darker the deeper they went.

Lane thought of grizzlies laired in this deep, and, quickly as he could, thought of something else. The Henry—Akins carried a cut-down trap-door Springfield—was more in the way than useful on the climb.

Lane had long ago learned to save himself when he had hard and then harder work to do, except when he was hauling cows out of sink-holes; he seemed ripe for damn foolishness around a sink-hole. Going down the steep rock face, thrusting the long barrel of the Henry muzzle-down through the back of his gunbelt to leave his hands free, Lane reminded himself of the climb yet to come once they'd crossed the canyon. Riding boots weren't the best sort of footwear for climbing among rocks; Lane had to pay attention where he set his feet down—that, or have a fine, strong hold on some little pine tree in case he slipped.

It seemed to him that Akins and he were making considerable noise climbing down, though likely the thick wall of pine behind them muffled the scrambling noises. The wind would be getting up, too, as evening came on. That would help.

Akins was below him now, climbing a little faster. Once he looked up, peering through the gathering dark, to see how Lane was doing. Akins climbed easily, with an odd, swinging sort of rythm from this pine tree to that, this rock ledge down to the next. Like a bear, or an African ape.

It occurred to Lane that it would be as well not to fight the marshal hand to hand, if it could be avoided. The man looked to be as strong as a steam engine . . . and young, too.

Now, they were deep into the canyon, getting near the bottom. The steep sides of the wash had begun to shallow out; the crowding pines were mostly trunk now, a gloomy, thick forest of lodge-poles, slender and straight. The foliage formed a roof over them thirty or forty feet thick, soft, dark, and green as only many-shaded green could be.

It was hot under here.

Lane slipped, half skidded down a final graveled grade—the Spring floods must sometimes come roaring through the canyon in a flood. Those years would see the finish of the pines for a man's lifetime, the floods sweeping them away, tearing them into kindling wood . . .

No fist-fight with Akins. Not if he could help it.

Was a time he wouldn't have been so shy of a drag-out with a bull-shouldered boy. Was a time Lane would have found it a pleasure to show Akins a thing or two about rough-housing—bite, beat, kick and thumb.

Not now. His bones told him that in constant small ways. His bones and muscles . . .

Lane threaded through the lodge-pole trunks, working across the canyon floor alongside Akins. There were little birds down here, hundreds of them. They flew like locusts, with quick whirring sounds, all around them. Not much in the way of singing. A small chirp, here and there—and that was as well; unlikely the Indians wouldn't notice a bunch of birds yelling down in this canyon. Not much singing, but they flew in quick clouds from the path he and Akins were taking across. Small brown birds, with a white streak across their wings. You could see it when they flew.

Fighting that Englishman . . . *There* was a fist-fight, by God. Man says the English don't like to get their hands dirty doing rough work, should have squared off with that Englishman. A rough cob in a smooth ear.

Beat a cowboy with a bung-starter. A few other dandy dustups like that. And never cared for it. Never liked hitting a man in the face. Strange, how it seemed a nasty thing to do. Nastier than a killing sometimes, if it was a fair enough shoot-out.

This was a rough walk. Should be getting cooler now, with evening coming on, but not down here. The pines held the heat in. Be a relief to get up there and among those damn Indians.

They reached the opposite wall—and it was every bit as rough as the other had been—and this would be climbing up, not climbing down.

Lane wasn't looking forward to it. The two hundred dollars from Dowd wasn't looking like too much money at all now. A damn climb like this was worth two hundred dollars a month.

Akins went up the rock face like a monkey, and Lane set his teeth, tightened his gunbelt a notch to keep the Henry from sliding through and falling, and went right on up after him.

He tried to use his feet as much as he could, climbing. Getting good foot-holds and climbing up with those, rather than hauling himself up with his hands. It seemed a better way to do it. A man's legs are a lot stronger than his arms.

It worked pretty well, at least for the first few yards. Lane would grip a pine branch, or knotted root sticking out of the rock, then wait for a moment to find a place for his boot-sole. Then he'd step up on that little ledge, or crack in the rock, or whatever, push himself up that way, and then get a fresh grip to hang on to. It worked pretty well, but it didn't keep him from getting tired.

He got plenty tired.

Akins climbed above him and kept climbing. Lane thought of putting out all his strength and keeping up with him, but he decided against it. The only way to deal with Akins—if he had to be dealt with—was sure as shooting not by trying to out-boy him. Akins had the cards of youth; may as well admit that. No use being galled by it.

Well, it galled him anyway.

Lane was running sweat. When the hell did this day get cool down here? His arms were shaking from the strain of holding him up on the rock-face while he scraped around with the boot-toes, trying to find a rest to step up on.

By God, it would be a terrible thing if he just ran out of oats and got stuck up here, couldn't go up or down, had to whisper out for Akins to come climbing back down and help him.

Jesus . . . it didn't bear thinking of! Just bear down—and climb! Those Indians were going to smart for this little picnic, if there was a whole tribe of them up there!

There wasn't.
There were five.
Lane and Akins lay side by side in soft brush, a long stone's throw from the canyon edge. The sun had set below the peaks; the light seemed the soft gold of late afternoon, but slowly growing darker, nearer to dusk.

Lane and Akins had crawled from the canyon edge upwind of the fire, through tangled brush down to the Indian camp. Lane hoped it would be Indians; he'd look a jackass if it was only some drifters stealing beef for a feed.

They'd crawled down through the choke-cherries and brambles, with Lane glad enough to be out of that canyon that he didn't care for thorns, or sore knees and elbows, either. No trouble keeping even with Akins, now.

The scent of smoke had grown stronger as they worked their way down from the rim of the draw. There was a smell of roasting meat to it, too. "Broken Iron beef," Akins had whispered, grinning. It was the first smile Lane had seen on him. The heavy, square Mex-dark face had been softened by it; the young man's hard brown eyes had softened some, too.

That had been a tough stretch. Some damn plants with long, whippy branches grew close to the ground with rows of thorns down every branch. Lane had never seen them before that he knew of, but he surely saw them now. Those

83

thorns stung, even through his buckskin jacket. They snagged right through it, like a house cat's claws.

He and Akins had come through that and seen the camp, at least part of it, through a patch of scrub berry bushes. They'd lain up there then, Lane, for one, glad of the breather. The last yards up that canyon wall had been a trial, and no mistake.

Then they'd seen two people.

For a moment, Lane had thought they were white; they were dressed white, in a raggedy sort of way—torn slouch hats, dirt-black trousers, and no button shirts worn shirt-tails out.

"White men, by God," Akins whispered.

But they weren't. The next moment, Lane saw that—and didn't have to see it.

He felt it.

Bad Indians. It was a sort of humming in the air, a feeling about those people. You could almost hear it.

Lane had had real bad Indian trouble only once. Despite old Ned Buntline, a man could do well enough out West and never have real trouble with Indians if he had any luck at all.

Lane had had that sort of trouble once, a long time ago. Ran out of luck then. That bad luck had cost him a friend. Lud Chambers swung over a slow fire, head down. Must have hung there for hours as his hair smoldered, then slowly burned away. Scalp blackening, blistering, peeling off as his brains began to bake . . . Must have hung there, roped upside down from a pinon pine, hung there for hours, screaming until his brains cooked . . .

Arizona—a beautiful territory if you stayed clear of the White Mountains.

"Well, what the heck *are* they?"

Akins had felt it, too.

"Texas Indians, I think, maybe Comanche."

"Horse-wallop!" Akins said. "What would those people be doing way the heck up here?"

"Busted out and run out by MacKensie and the Army."

Another man had come to the fire to join the two. He was older. He squatted facing Lane, and Lane peered hard rather than make all the movement necessary to get the little telescope out. He squinted hard at the man's face.

"Not Comanche . . . I think they're Kiowa."

Akins grunted. "There's three of them," he said, and had no sooner said it, then two more came to the fire with rifles in their hands.

Five of them, with maybe one more out on guard. Horses would be staked out or hobbled just past the fire. Lane shifted slightly to try and see past the berry bushes. If he could get to those horses and fuss them, then sure as hell those riding-Indians would come barreling over to see what was up. Weren't about to lose those horses. They'd come running right into his gun. No sneaking around the brush after a scatter of Kiowas.

"I'm going for their horses," he whispered to Akins. "When the fuss starts, you come on in behind them. We'll take them front and back."

85

"Supposing there's a guard?" Akins was letting Lane call the play, but he wasn't going stupid, either. There was no way to plan for the guard; either there was one, or there wasn't. Indians had no rules about that. If there was another man out there, they'd have to fight him. Simple as that.

Certain sure, Lane had no intention of running off to climb back up and down that canyon. He'd done his climbing. From here, it was going to be Indian pony and the long way back. No more climbing.

"If there is a guard, we'll kill him, too."

Akins nodded. It appeared to be the sort of agreement he was accustomed to. "Okay."

Lane could hear the Indians laughing about something over at the fire. They had sticks leaning up at an angle to the flames, chunks of beef stuck on them, cooking. Four of the Kiowas looked like men grown; one of them was older than the other three. That one looked to have no teeth at all. Had a nose on him, though. Big nose. It was that made Lane feel they were Kiowas, that and their size. The Comanches were a slight-built people.

The fifth Indian looked to be a boy—skinny and dark-complexioned as a nigger. Quite a note on *him*, too. It was too far to make out from their expressions what the joke was all about, whether they were telling stories, or not. People thought Indians had no sense of humor, but they did. Indians were always laughing about something. Lane had heard that Chinamen were always laughing, too, when white people weren't around. Likely both were laughing at the whites.

"Say—look at that," Akins whispered to him. "They got a sissy with them."

The boy had bent over to tend the cooking meat, and the older man had leaned forward and grabbed his butt. One of the other men said something, and they all laughed, the boy, too. The older man slipped a hand down into the front of the boy's trousers. The boy stayed there, and let him do it.

"Don't that beat all," Akins said. "They brought a sissy with them!"

"Could be," Lane said. "Could be that's a girl, too. Kiowa girls go raiding just like the men sometimes, if they're tomboys and not married yet."

"That's a sissy," Akins said.

"Well, the Indians have as many of those as anybody else does." Lane thought he'd take the Henry along, use it for his first shot, maybe the second. Use the Bisley for the rest. And hoping that Akins was as good as he was cracked up to be. Five to two was odds—and maybe a horse guard to boot.

"Wait 'till the fuss—then you come quick," he said. Took his Stetson off, put it down in the grass, and began to crawl off to the left.

"Quick as a wink," Akins said.

Sure as hell, he was earning Dowd's pay today.

Where there weren't briars, there were flint stones sharp as carving knives. Lane didn't dare raise his backside up to a full crawl; he low-crawled all the way, dragging himself along with his arms and elbows. He could feel the blood soaking his jacket where his elbows were cut and bleeding.

87

It was a long way to go—out far enough to the left of that fire that five Kiowa Indians wouldn't see him or hear him. A long way to go, and a slow way to go it.

Had to pray the horses were back in the trees, and not in his path. Some stomp and whinny before he was set, and he'd be in a pickle. The Henry was giving him fits, jammed down the back of his gunbelt. He'd tried crawling with the damned thing across his arms, the way soldiers did and the only result of that had been a couple of rattles on rocks, steel to stone, loud enough for the Kiowa to have heard if they hadn't been so busy funning. The mountains did that to flatlanders, had done that to him when he'd first come up in them—made men feel they didn't have to worry about other men. The mountains made every other thing, even trouble, look small.

He'd tried the rifle a little further and got another loud "click" against a stone for his trouble. Then the Henry had gone barrel-first down his gunbelt. It made crawling tougher, but quieter. The damn thing . . . And the light was starting to go, too.

His elbows were near worn out, when he saw the horses standing in a bunch beneath two tall larch trees. Looked to be slip-knot hobbled. And not Indian ponies, either. Ranch horses—white people's horses. The Kiowa must have eaten their ponies after they stole these nice grain-feds.

Lane saw no guard near them.

He turned his head slowly, and glanced through the grass stems at the Indians. They were eating the roasted beef, getting up to slice more of it off the fire-sticks. The skinny boy was wearing only his shirt—the older man must have made him take his pants off. It was a boy, all right—no girl come raiding.

Lane began to work his way toward the horses, heading for the nearer of the two larches. He was getting tired of being on his belly. Halfway there, about five yards off, he saw one of the horses turn its head to look at him. It was a scrawny bay with a scarred chest. Apparently it hadn't seen many men crawling through high grass. It seemed interested in that . . . watched Lane with close attention as he crawled nearer. Another of the horses noticed him, a small pinto. It shifted and crow-hopped a step away, forelegs straining at its hobbles.

The string was running out. Time to open the ball.

Lane was too glad to be getting up on his feet to be worried. There was something about hunting people, even dangerous people, that made you feel you had the better of them. It could be a dangerous feeling.

He dragged the Henry up out of his gunbelt and climbed to his feet. He marked the oldest of the Kiowa, levered a round into the Henry's receiver —and dove back down into the grass under a storm of fire.

Never even got off a shot! It was the quickest he'd ever seen a bunch of people react. Lane scurried for the larch with bullets smacking and humming past him. One rifle round tore a small chunk from the larch's trunk just as he got to it.

The horses were screaming; one must have been hit—damn lot of shooting!

He tucked in behind the tree trunk and then threw the Henry down. He looked out to the right, ducked a shot coming in at him, then switched sides and looked to the left. One of the Kiowa was coming for him in a rapid stooped run. He had a busted-stock double-barrel shotgun, and fired one barrel at Lane as he came. The shot tore at the tree above Lane's head, and he drew the Bisley, fired at the man who was very close, and hit him low in the belly.

The Kiowa went to one knee, fired the second barrel, and pitched over onto his face. Lane shot him again, down through his shoulder into his body, and the man heaved up and onto an elbow, trying to reload the shotgun. Lane shot him through the side of the head, and the Indian sneezed blood and died.

A bullet burned the inside of Lane's right forearm, and he rolled out into the grass and shot a Kiowa firing at him with some sort of big revolver. The bullet hit the man high in the middle of his chest, and knocked him down and killed him.

Lane got up on one knee to see better over the powder smoke, and reload. He got up and flipped the Bisley's gate open and was hit by a man come flying at him like a devil.

There was a smell and force, a strength different from a white man's. A quick, all-out kind of strength. Lane felt the cold and twisted hard away from the knife's edge; he didn't know where it had cut him. He got his hand down to his right boot—

his revolver was gone, knocked away from him—
found the handle of the toothpick, pulled the blade
free and struck at the Indian's side as they rolled.
The blade turned on a bone and nearly sprained
Lane's wrist. The Indian's face came near his and
he looked into the man's eyes for an instant.
Nothing there but great effort, black, squinting,
full of effort. Lane flailed to find the man's right
arm, found it and gripped it as hard as he could.
He struck with the toothpick again, and the blade
went in.

The Indian grunted and kicked free. Kicked and
kicked, caught Lane in the guts and the side of the
head, and kicked himself free. As he jumped back,
up on his feet, Lane lunged after him, seized his
ankle and tripped him. The Indian fell, then spun
up onto his hands and knees and Lane reached
over and drove the toothpick into the center of the
man's back.

He drove it in as he were driving a railway spike
into timber. The nine-inch double-edged blade
sank to the hilt.

The Kiowa gasped at the blow, and tried to
stand up, but Lane wouldn't let go the knife handle
and was hauled half up with him. There was a
noise then, and a bag of wet struck him hard in the
face and stung him. It was in his eyes.

The Indian convulsed and fell over sideways,
and Lane, half blind, fell with him. He looked up,
blinking, and saw Akins staring down at him. He
had his big, black English revolver in his hand.
Smoke was drifting from it.

Akins looked at the knife handle sticking up out

91

of the Kiowa's back. "Your nigger, I guess," he
said. "I put the other two down over there." He
watched while Lane got his bandanna out of his
back pocket and wiped the brains and mess off his
face.

"Sorry," he said, with the second smile Lane had
seen on him, and started to say something more,
when Lane saw his face change. There was hardly
time to say what the change had been, because
Akins suddenly turned as swiftly as a shuttle in a
steam-mill—facing Lane one instant, turned away
the next—and fired a shot off into the brush,
standing as straight as a man at the Springfield
Match.

The brush where he had shot thrashed, and a
small branch broke. A man in there, a Kiowa, was
trying to breathe with a crushed lung, making a
snoring, tearing sound. Akins fired again, the
English revolver bucking high, and the snoring
sound stopped.

It was exceptional shooting, a thirty-yard shot if
it was an inch. Lane saw that Akins was a man who
had to be fought up close. Must have been many a
rough in Fort Smith who'd gone out into the street
to face Segrue's young deputy, started toward
Akins to get close enough for good shooting, and
was hit and dying before he'd stepped a yard.

It would have to be close-up, with Akins or not
at all.

Lane wiped the last of the mess off of his face,
wishing for a run to splash the filth off in. He
dropped his bandanna in the grass and picked up
the Bisley. He felt that his hands were shaking,

92

but didn't glance down for fear Akins would see it. Instead, he said, "Good shooting," and ambled off toward the place Akins had made that long shot at. The horse guard must have wandered off, heard the commotion, and come back to take an ambush shot if he could. Akins must have seen the slightest movement way off there to the right, some movement of the leaves, and that was enough for him.

Fast the boy might or might not be, but sure, he certainly was.

Lane found the Kiowa dead, tangled in his death agony amongst the branches of the bush he'd hidden under. He'd been a tall man, with smallpox scars on his face, and a finger missing from his left hand. Akins' bullets had both taken him in the chest. Remarkable shooting. Match-grade shooting, that was for sure.

The Indian's rifle lay beside him. It was a Sharps.

A beauty. .50 caliber, folding range-sights, and a stock decorated with rows of silver nail heads.

Lane picked it up, helfted it. Beautiful. It was a rifle he wanted. The Kiowa had a belt of cartridges around his waist. The original owner had taken fine care of the piece. Must have been a little slow, though, when these Kiowas came by, just a little too slow.

Lane took the rifle and cartridges back into the camp clearing. He felt blood running down his left side, where the Kiowa had knifed him, and stopped to pull up his jacket and shirt to see the wound.

There were two cuts down his ribs, one deep

enough so that a bit of the white bone could be seen where his skin stretched over the rib. The cuts were starting to burn considerable, but the bleeding was nothing much. The cuts would do, if he got to water soon enough and washed them out for a while.

His stomach hurt him, too, where the Indian had kicked him. That had been a fierce man . . .

Lane didn't see Akins and as he turned to look by the Kiowas' camp fire, he heard someone screaming.

A thin, squealing scream, like a trapped rabbit's cry before it was picked up and its neck broken.

Lane stooped to put the Sharps down—a fine piece, but he'd never fired it—and drew the Bisley. Surely to God, they hadn't missed *two* of the damn people!

He heard the cry again, past the campfire, toward the canyon rim, and started that way, trotting, keeping to the larches as well as he could. He got to the campfire—the beef was burning—and stopped to listen.

No sound at all now.

"Akins!"

Lane thought he heard a movement to the left . . . something stirring. Evening was coming on fast. The light was almost gone.

"Akins!"

He heard a stirring, then nothing.

Off to the left.

Lane went toward it, his side burning at him with every step. When he pushed some brush aside, he heard Akins' voice, sounding strange.

94

"Don't come in here."

"Like hell," Lane said, put his head down and drove through thick brambles. He tugged and kicked his way thorugh—and came upon Harley Akins, on his feet in the thicket, just fastening his trousers.

The Kiowa boy lay naked in the brush, on his belly, his skinny legs spread wide. The boy's asshole was stretched open, wet with what Akins had left there. The boy had a streak of blood along the side of his head, in the thick black hair, and his throat had been cut.

He was still alive, just barely, making a gargling sound in his throat, drowning in his own blood. Akins had sliced his throat wide open. White tendons and things showed in the red.

Lane shot the boy, and killed him.

Then he turned and pushed his way through the brambles out of there. He didn't care to think too much about Akins doing the boy that way. It had been a savage thing, but Lane had known many sissies, nice people, for the most part, and if they liked a boy, now and then—well, an old pimp had not much moral ground to stand on.

What concerned him more was that Akins had planned it all, and very quickly, in the middle of a fight.

Lane had seen him shoot for keeps, and that skill meant that Akins had wanted the boy, and deliberately grazed him across the head to put him down until he had time to get back to him. That was cold thinking, and fine shooting, and it showed Akins a wonderfully dangerous man.

Lane reloaded the Bisley, and stood waiting for Akins to come out of the brush. If Akins was ashamed, it would likely come to shooting.

Akins came out of the brambles in that slow, steady way of his, paying the thorns no heed. He was wiping the blade of a folding Barlow knife on his sleeve; he had the boy's scalp in his other hand. No shame, and no shooting, then.

"I found a fine Sharps over there, by the one you killed," Lane said. "I'd like to buy that rifle off you."

"Oh, heck—take the thing," Akins said, and snapped the scalp in the air to flip the blood off it. "It's yours."

"I think not," Lane said. "I'll pay for it."

And they said nothing more to each other during the long ride around the canyon and back down the mountain in moonlight. Although Akins sang a song, once: "Step Up, My Ladies."

FIVE

THEY PARTED at the Forks, Akins waving himself away without a word, leading the string of stolen horses behind him as he rode. They'd stopped up at Bull Pond an hour away from the mountain, and Lane had been glad to get down from the pinto, strip, and wash off in the still, cold water. The pond water was black as pitch in the moonlight, but Lane was happy enough, getting the bits of dried stuff off him, and out of his hair, and washing the cuts on his side.

Akins had sat his horse while Lane washed, pulled a pipe and fixings from his saddlebag, lit up, and sat blowing a cloud. Lane supposed Akins had taken to the pipe to make himself seem older.

Lane had washed, then come out, dressed, and mounted, and they'd ridden almost another hour to the Forks and separated there, Akins taking the stolen horses on into Grover.

In all that ride, Akins had not said a word, though he'd seemed easy enough, and friendly. He sat the saddle easier, too. Perhaps doing the Kiowa boy that way had eased him.

Still, Lane was pleased to be parted from Akins. He was tired of figuring the best way to kill the boy if it ever came to a fight between them. This sort of figuring was something Lane had always done when he met a fighting man. It stood him in good stead more often than not, but it made him feel poorly just the same.

Close up, was the way to kill Akins—or try to kill him. Close up, and call him a "sissy for one-eye." It might make him awkward . . .

Lane guided the pinto down along the Little Chicken and then across it, splashing the shallows into silver in the moonlight. It was a pretty night, not too warm or cool. Dawn only a few hours away, now. Too early to wake Dowd up with the news about the Indians. Would be big drinking in Grover over this—a little Indian war of their own, right up here in the Rockies. Akins the hero of it, natural enough. A town marshal who didn't puff himself as a fighter was bound to have more trouble than otherwise from common drunks and such. Fight would do Akins a lot of good—Kiowas, too. Would sound like something, for sure.

They'd left the Indians up there to rot, something Lane had not cared to do and had never done before, if he could help it. And he knew why he hadn't pushed the matter with Akins. He hadn't wanted to be seeing that throat-cut boy, surely not having Akins and him handling the boy.

That was the nasty thing. May as well admit it.

Spoiled the fight, in a way. And what was too bad, because those redmen had fought just fine. They'd have killed any ordinary two white men who'd troubled them, that was for sure. Remarkable quick off their marks. You'd never see a bunch of white men so quick to fight all together. White men would have been yelling, running around like barnyard geese, trying to get set.

Only a few miles into headquarters now. Broken Iron was a big spread, but a lot of it was steep ups and downs. Lane thought he might stay up and have breakfast instead of going to bed at all. He was tired, but not so tired he had to sleep. Wasn't that old yet.

As he rode, he reached down into his right boot, and drew the Arkansas toothpick. When he'd cleaned the knife up at the pond, he'd feared he felt a nick in the edge of the blade. Hate to have to have that ground out; even at best, it tended to take some of the temper out of that place.

He looked at the bright blade by moonlight— long, slim, almost delicate looking. The knife had won fights for him more times than he could easily remember. The last time, more than a year before —almost two years, now—he'd killed a madman with it. A woman-murderer . . . The fellow was mad as a hatter; still, he'd deserved his end.

There was no nick in the edges of the blade. They still had the fine, furry sort of feeling under the thumb. Sharp enough to shave with. To close-shave with.

Many didn't care for a double-edged knife, claimed it made the blade too weak for work. Pre-ferred Bowies, or some such sturdier weapons. Lane had never found the toothpick too weak for his sort of work. For camp work, a man should use a light ax anyway. Only a fool used a fine blade for that sort of thing.

Thought he might have injured it though, jamming it down into the Kiowa in that fashion. That had been rough work.

Perhaps he was tired enough for a little shut-eye, just an hour or so.

He rode down to headquarters more than an hour later. Bucky Vaughn had challenged him a few minutes over the Little Chicken, so Broken Iron wasn't dead asleep. Bucky was up, and the night-herd over in the west Breaks.

Another hour and more 'till dawn, but the hands would be piling out soon enough. Lane thought he'd stop at Cookie's for a bite, then sack in. Dowd was never up before seven in the morning, anyway. Owner's privilege.

Lane rode past the main house—one storey log and rock, nothing fancy—and past the corrals to the bunk house. He and Tom Shand, Dowd's foreman, shared a boarded off room at the far end.

Shand was an odd one for a ranch foreman, a small, fat fellow, and very pleasant company. Knew a lot about cows, and men, too, Lane supposed. Had spotted Lane's ways soon enough when the Gupp boys looked to be making trouble, showing the regulator he wasn't such hot horse shit after all.

When he'd seen that trouble coming, Shand had only asked Lane not to kill those boys. Then he'd butted out. Lane wouldn't have killed them, anyway. Killing drovers, unless you just couldn't help it, was close to murder. Cowboys were mighty ignorant, and they worked too hard, most of them, to ever get really handy with weapons.

A lot of men had made easy reputations, killing drovers.

So when the proper time came, Lane had struck Jake Gupp across the head with a fence-board, and calmed him. The Gupp boys had been good company after that.

Shand had been all right. Not afraid of Lane but not too friendly with him, not trying to pretend to be rough, either. A damned good cattle-man, too, for all his size and fat.

Lane put the pinto up in the lower stable, rubbed him down, and grained him. The pinto was a good horse, strong and nice tempered. The other men left the pinto to him.

Shand was asleep, but woke when Lane put his saddle-bags down in the room's far corner.

"Say, now." Shand propped himself up on one elbow on his bunk. He looked a good deal like an owl—round, grey-stubbled face, sparse hair sticking up every which way. "What luck with those rustlers?"

"Sorry to wake you," Lane said. "Indians."

"Are you funning me?"

"I am not," Lane said. "Six out-of-country Kiowa. Or they seemed like Kiowa to me."

"By god, you *are* funning—and damn early in the morning!"

"No, sir, I'm not. Indians."

Shand sat up and yawned. "Jumpin' Jesus!

That's the biggest news in this neck of the woods since Hector was a pup. You catch any of those Texas redskins?"

"Killed them. I went up with Akins. He killed some, too."

Shand had nothing to say to this. He sat and looked at Lane, an odd expression on his face. Then he said, "Poor devils."

Lane had the Sharps over on his bunk, was sitting with the big rifle on his lap, looking it over. Grey light was falling through the dusty little window between their cots. Lane thought, not for the first time, that Shand was a decent man. No part of the bully about him.

"Yes," he said, "that's right." He worked the action on Sharps. Akins had made a gesture of refusing the three twenty dollar gold pieces Lane handed to him up at Bull Pond, for the rifle. But Lane had held the money out until Akins took it. It was a lot of money for an old rifle—more, probably, than the piece was worth. Still, it looked pretty good to him, now that he could see in in daylight. The Kiowa had either cared for it and kept it clean and oiled or he hadn't had it long. It was in fine order. "It's true they didn't have much of a chance."

"Not against the two of you," Shand said. "I would say not much change for them, there."

It nettled Lane a little, and he said, "There were six of them."

Shand grunted, got up, and walked across the room, through the door there, and into the drover's side. Lane heard him yelling the cowboys up out of their soogins, getting them up for work. "Blister you, Benny Wallop—stop foolin' with your ab-do-man an' get out of that sack!" Soon enough, the cowboys were up, grumbling and stomping into their boots first thing.

Lane had wanted to go over to the cook shack, have a bite of breakfast, but he decided not. Didn't care to be telling adventure stories to the cowpokers. They'd be talking Indians as fast as they could clear their mouths of cornbread and fried eggs. He'd report to Dowd about it, let the others make up the yarns they chose. Had had enough troubles with reputation to want more up here on the Iron.

Akins was welcome to the glory of this fight.

Lane wondered if he'd be able to sleep. Had had trouble sleeping, sometimes, after a fight. He got up off the cot, stood the Sharps up in the corner near the head of his bunk, shucked his gunbelt, and took off his boots and clothes. Thought he might have to put his boots on again to go out and pee, then decided he didn't have to.

He rolled into his blankets, and stretched out with a sigh. Damn sure he'd be stiff as a post when he got up. He could feel the ache in his muscles from the fighting, and the ride—the climbing, most of all. The whole damn evening and night had worn him out. The cuts hurt him, too. Little things like that hurt him more and more. Have to get Cookie to give them a look'n see some time today. Didn't want a sepsis there, that was for sure.

Shand came in, went over to his little foot-trunk, and started to get dressed. He looked over at Lane

103

and said, "No offense, on those Indians."

"No offense, Mister Shand," Lane said. "Though they were fierce enough, most of them. We might have chased them off, I suppose, but they made a fight of it."

Shand sighed, and put on his shirt. "We've finished those people," he said. "And it's a shame."

"Civilization, Mister Shand," Lane said. "Civilization." He turned over on his bunk, and closed his eyes to sleep.

Shand was quiet about the rest of his dressing and about his going out of the room, but Lane hadn't fallen asleep. He kept his eyes closed so that he wouldn't have to talk any more. That ex-Mountie, Whistler, had the right idea about talking. It caused more trouble than anything.

He thought he might be dreaming, but he wasn't sure. Sometimes, when he was asleep and dreaming, he knew it. Then if he wanted to, he could fly as high as any hawk and know it was a dream, all the time.

Now, though, he wasn't certain. The country was mountains, and there were Indians in it, riding along like in a painting in a fine saloon. Feathered war-bonnets and white buckskins with porcupine fringe and beadwork all over. No Diggers, that was for sure. Sioux or Cheyenne. Maybe Crows, from their good looks and finery . . . Crow Indians, he supposed, going to some big feast or celebration.

He'd thought he'd try to fly, in case it was a

dream, fly up in the air, look at the whole bunch of them, see if there were any good-looking women with them.

But he couldn't. He could glide along the ground in a way, hardly touching. But he couldn't get higher than that. He assumed then, that it wasn't a dream.

One of the Indians, one that didn't look so nice—an old one with a dirty face and a big nose—turned his pony and come over to Lane and said, "Good morning."

"Good morning," Lane said, polite as if he were in a drawing room.

"What are you doing here?" the old man said, speaking as good English as a Christian.

"I'm Buckskin Frank Leslie," Lane said to him. "And I'm hiding out here. A man has come from Texas."

But the old Indian didn't hear him. He just sat on his horse and nodded and said, "Good morning."

Lane woke with a jolt.

Matthew Dowd stood looking down at him. Bright morning sunlight shone into the room. Clouds of tiny dust-specks smoked in the light.

"Good morning," Dowd said. "You're a heavy sleeper, Mister Lane. And from all reports, have every right to be." The sunlight reflected gold in his pinch-nose spectacles.

Lane threw the blankets aside and sat up on the edge of the bunk. He was sorry that Dowd had seen him sleeping.

"I'll get up and come up to the house," he said.

Dowd went over and sat down on Shand's bunk. "No need for that," he said. "Take your ease—you've had quite a night, I believe."

Lane got up, took clean clothes off a plank shelf, and started to get dressed. He didn't care for Dowd sitting there watching him.

"Seth Bailey rode over from Three-spot just now," Dowd said. "Says there's a great deal of talk in town this morning about Marshal Akins having killed a number of Indians. You apparently having helped him in that." Dowd nodded to himself, pleased with his two-hundred-dollar investment, Lane supposed. Lane sat down to pull on his boots.

Shand then had said nothing to the ranch people about the fight. Lane regretted the breakfast he might have had. His belly was about as sore from hunger as the rest of him from effort and abuse.

"The marshal and you, Mister Lane, have performed a considerable service. Something the sheep people, of course, were unwilling to help in."

Lane doubted anyone had asked Parris's people for help. More than likely assumed the herders had done the killings. Done the steer-butchering, anyway.

"It's a very good mark to the account of Broken Iron," Dowd said, nodding to himself again. The little man was dressed like an Englishman—low-heeled riding boots, tuck-in pants and all. Sitting on the edge of Shand's bunk, Dowd's boot-soles barely reached the floor. General Tom Thumb, for sure.

Dowd sat looking at him, his eyeglasses reflecting light. Lane had never known Dowd to speak of anything not relating to his cattle business here, or up in Canada. He supposed the little man to have other concerns but had never heard him talk about them.

Dowd had offered his congratulations but he was still sitting on Shand's bunk. That meant there was more business to be discussed.

Lane buckled his gunbelt on, picked up his hat, and stood waiting for Dowd to say his say. Lane wanted his breakfast.

Dowd took off his spectacles, pulled a white handkerchief from the breast pocket of his jacket, and commenced polishing the little round lenses.

"Mister Lane," he said, still polishing—it was *Mister* Lane, now—"I have some information regarding that Texan person that the sheep people have brought into the community." He put his spectacles on and tucked the handkerchief back into his jacket pocket. "This bravo is named Frank Pace, it seems. Have you ever heard of this man, Mister Lane? You must more, I suppose, in somewhat similar circles."

Frank Pace . . . Parris and the sheep-herders must have decided to fight all out.

Pace . . . Yes, indeed, Lane had heard of him. Never met the man, but heard of him, and more than once. Supposed to be the finest gun out of Texas, now that Hardin was in the penetentiary and Allison dead of an accidental broken neck.

Pace had had a fight with Allison, Lane thought —had heard of that, anyway. Both of them hurt in the shooting. That said everything that needed to be said, to have fought with Clay Allison, and come out alive.

The hardest case in Texas. They didn't come harder. And young. Younger than Mister Lane, that was for sure.

"I know of him," Lane said.

"Well . . . " Dowd said, "there you are. He's the fellow we have to beat. Beat him, and Parris and the rest will turn tail soon enough."

We. Lane was amused by that *we.* He'd heard that sort of talking many, many times, by people who were paying him to fight other people. He'd heard all of this before. It wearied him to listen to it. Next, sure as shooting, Dowd would give him advice on how to call this Pace out and put him down.

"It seems to me," Dowd said, "that it would be best for you to confront this hoodlum in Grover."

No more *we.*

"There, at least, Marshal Akins will see fair play."

Would have been funny, if Lane were hearing it all for the first time. *Akins see fair play . . .* That was a good one. No marshal worth his salt could ever let two prime gunmen shoot it out in his town and let the winner simply ride off, to come back around town whenever he chose.

No marshal worth his salt. And whatever else he might be, Harley Akins was sure enough salty.

Lane wondered if Pace had heard yet who was marshal of Grover. Must have, by now. It would be a little fat in the fire for him, that was for sure. It

108

began to look like everybody'd be earning their money now.

"I'm going to go get some breakfast, Mister Dowd," Lane said, and walked to the door. He was tired of standing there before the owner, with his hat in his hand. And he was hungry.

"Wait a minute," Dowd called after him, but Lane went on out into the drovers' room, crossed it, and went outside. He heard the little man trotting after him.

Dowd caught up with him in the yard beside the pump. Lane pumped a dollop and washed his face. Needed a shave. He thought he'd have breakfast, first—getting late morning, by the light—then come back in and shave.

"Mister Lane," Dowd said at the pump, panting a little from his trot, "the Gupp brothers have been murdered down at Faraway." Lane dried his face with the same dirty towel that had been hanging at the pump since he'd hired on.

"Who by?" he said.

"Apparently murdered by the Texan, Pace. Supposedly he came upon a quarrel they were having with the Porter girl and murdered them out of hand." Dowd nodded, as if it were just what he might have expected.

Lane could imagine the quarrel might have waxed mighty hot. Still, the news was a jolt. The Gupps had been nothing much, but Jake, at least, had had some sand. Might have been handy in a fight . . .

Pace had come onto trouble, and stepped right

109

in. A strange thing for a professional to do. Lane wondered if the Porter girl had had something to do with it. Maybe this Pace fancied himself as a rescuer of ladies in distress.

Good news, if true—that he was so foolish.

Good news.

Not that he didn't know another fool liable to do the same sort of thing. Fellow called himself Lane, now.

———————

Cookie was not pleased to be asked for a late breakfast. The news of the fight had gotten around for sure, but had not impressed McCorkle.

McCorkle—Cookie—was a young man, and a dire drinker. Liked to say he'd drunk his teeth right out of his head—which he might have, having none, but still ate everything, tough steak and hard biscuit and all, chewing the food with great hard face-folding munches of his jaws. "Gums as hard as any man's teeth," he'd brag around a wet, mashed mouthful.

Door nail drunks were not tolerated around most ranches; McCorkle was because he could cook. And not just in volume, which was the province of all ranch cooks, but in taste. McCorkle cooked good food, one of his secrets being that he refused to use trash stuff in his cooking. Had a young cowpoker to pick over the beans before he boiled them, chose his own steer to slaughter, instead of taking any dying animal the foreman might pick out for the cook-shed, and would put no coffee beans to grind that hadn't come right out of St. Louis, Missouri, and the Great Atlantic and Pacific Tea Company.

The result of all this care was good eats. And on those days when McCorkle's weakness overcame him, the hands would select out one of their own to do their best.

Dowd had nothing to do with this, and didn't mind, since he and his wife were done and cooked for by a fat Sauk woman they'd brought down from Canada. Whistler, the ex-Mountie, ate at their table.

So it was that when Lane had finally shaken Dowd loose—needing time to be let alone to think, and needing his breakfast even more—he sat himself down at the long, dirty plank table, and set himself to listen to a few minutes of complaint by McCorkle about latecomers and owner's kiss-butts who expected special service at all hours, no matter what.

Lane listened, said he was sorry, and watched McCorkle begin to shuffle his frying pans, slice beef liver and bacon, crack eggs, and pull a handful of this morning's biscuits from his gravy sack.

Ten minutes later, Lane was eating a breakfast good enough for the Waldorf Hotel in New York—or almost.

He tucked in to a half-pound of liver, cooked pink—an old San Francisco taste—a stack of bacon slices, three open-eye eggs, and four big biscuits and butter. That, and three tin cups of coffee and brown sugar. More food than Lane had

had an appetite for lately; but he was hungry enough now and put every bit of it away.

McCorkle who, like all cooks, liked big feeders, then went out of his way to offer Lane a piece of apple pie, and was insulted when Lane turned it down as a belly-popper.

It was a most satisfactory meal, and Lane felt considerable better when he left the cook-shed and walked out by the corrals. Only thing he might have wanted was a fine cigar. There had been a time he'd had plenty of those—the finest Cubans. And only a week's ride from here, at that.

He leaned against a corral fence, watching Wiley Liss flap-break a colt. The old wrangler was bent as a beer-garden pretzel from breaks and busts off broncs, but he had a light hand for a green horse. Give Dowd credit, he held nice horse-flesh. Wouldn't stand for abuse, either. Of course, that was a matter of money, likely, more than kindness.

Wiley was talking to the colt, talking to it about a baseball game, sounded like, and walking around the animal flapping a saddle blanket at it. Colt didn't care for that, at all. Kept trying to shy and being caught up by the snubbing post. Wiley was taking it easy though, not pushing too hard. In a while, in a few hours, the cold would stand still for him, and the old wrangler would flap and wave the blanket, and talk about baseball right at the horse's face, and the colt not bat an eye.

A beautiful day. More and more, despite the fierce winters, Lane was happiest in high mountain country. Some Eastern writer once described fine air as being just like wine. It was true of this air, true of the mountain air, for sure.

Lane supposed that girl was long married. Some smart fellow taking care of her, managing a hotel. And quite a thing to manage, at that. The English put it very well. Not Lane's cup of tea. It wouldn't have done. It wouldn't have done at all. He'd have broken Sarah's heart with his foolishness and violence, even if old Buntline could have kept his mouth shut.

Better this way. Years gone by, now. And better so.

What a wonderful draw that Shannon fellow had had. Good enough to put Slim Wilson down. Good enough to lay a scar across Lane's face for keep, too.

That had been a time and no mistake. And fine cigars, to boot.

Wiley was up close to the colt now, breathing in its nostrils. Worked with some horses—didn't work with others. The colt's ears were laid back flat, whites showing all around the pupils of its eyes. Wiley was wasting his time with that card.

Lane decided to go in and shave, then cut out a mount—let the pinto rest a day—and go on into town. Might go to Mrs. Phelps, and talk to the Porter girl about that fight at Faraway.

Might meet Pace, too. Pace would have heard about Dowd's regulator, and the little Indian fight.

Might meet Frank Pace. See what the fellow was like.

It was not his usual way of doing, heading straight into a fight. It puzzled Lane that he felt like riding right into town. Not that he was so damn confident he could kill the Texan, either. Fact was, it might well go the other way. Pace had years on him and a fearful name.

Might well go the other way . . .

Lane thought perhaps he might be badly scared and rushing the fight because of that. It was more than likely so.

He considered it, while staring into Shand's cracked shaving mirror, a cut-throat in his hand, scraping at his chin-bristles. Have to be careful up around the scar. The thin, dead-white line angled across his left cheek was slow to heal were it injured.

Lane considered whether he was afraid of this Texican, and decided he must be. Of course, there had been a time when he wouldn't have been, when the news that a deadly fellow had come to town would have set him in his saddle with a yelp and it would have been heigh-ho and away we go! to town, and a shooting the moment the naughty fellow showed.

Damn sure he could use that wild young fighter now—could use the loss of ten or twenty years. Pace would damn sure think he'd met a steam-saw then, by God!

A little faster on the draw then, for sure. Had to be. Though Lane had not noticed getting slower with a revolver in the past years. Seemed to him he'd held his speed pretty well. Fooling himself, likely. As for the other ways of fighting, no use pretending about that. The Kiowa that had wrestled with him up on the mountain had been stronger and faster. Hadn't been as good with a knife as he should have been, though, considering he was Indian. But he'd sure been stronger and faster. Come on Lane like a race horse—knocked him ass over tea-kettle—and if he'd thrown his knife away, would likely have beat the tar out of one has-been famous fighting man.

It was as well that he still had some speed with a revolver. For damn sure his days as a knock-down-and-drag-outer were coming to an end.

He finished his shave, wiped the soap from his face with half an old towel, and rinsed the razor in the basin. Of course, he could always try and stay out of tights. Selling his gunhand to people like Dowd was no way at all to do that.

No way at all.

He walked out of the bunk-house and down toward the corrals, feeling the slight sting of the sun's heat where the razor had scraped his skin.

Soon enough, in a few short years, he'd start to look like a mighty strange sort of a hard-case, a moss-horn, would be what he'd look like. Hadn't happened yet, of course. Not for a few years.

But looking in a shaving mirror, you could see it coming.

At the corrals, he cut out a rangy bay with a blaze on his forehead called Roscoe, and a sidling pain in the butt he was, but strong and fast. Lane caught him first throw, snubbed and saddled him; then led him out, mounted, and rode him up to the bunk-house to get his rifle and saddle-bags. Lane

thought of riding by the cook-shack to beg a sandwich for his nooner, then remembered he'd
refused McCorkle's offer of a piece of his apple
pie, and decided he'd be wasting his time.

He brought out the Sharps—the stock and
receiver stuck up high out of the bucket—and
strapped the big rifle alongside the cantle. Lane
had known men who preferred to carry their rifles
alongside the back of their saddles, worrying
they'd knock some teeth out on the stock, ducking
branches, if the rifle sheath was strapped up front.

Lane thought a man who forgot where he kept
his rifle, should have a tooth or two knocked out to
remind him.

Now he was ready to travel.

He swung up, settled into the leather, and
booted the bay out into a line suited to cut the
Little Chicken five miles out from headquarters.

A cowpoker named Billy Betts coming in, met
and passed him with a word or two about Indian
fighting, and Lane was courteous to him and
agreed that Akins was a heller with knife and
pistol; that it was something to have seen; and that
he was lucky to have had a crack at the Redskins
at all in such company.

The bay was fresh, and, once Billy Betts had
passed, Lane let the horse out in a run. It was one
of Dowd's rules that Iron horses were not to be
run except on orders or chousing cattle. It was a
sensible rule, and most good ranches held to it,
but Lane had always run a horse whenever he felt
the wish and had not been interfered with about it
by anyone, foreman or owner, on any of the

spreads he'd worked, even when he was trying to play drover for eats and a bunk.

The bay paused in running to sidle and half-buck, and Lane smacked the horse fore and aft just as quick—fore with the ends of the reins, aft with his Stetson.

He'd never cared for horsemen who seemed to need a whip to stay on a troublesome horse, like the fellows always carrying dog whips and stock whips. Have to have something in their hands.

He could feel the shallow cuts the Kiowa had given him working as he rode. Should have let McCorkle give them a look'n see, but in the shaving mirror they'd seemed to be clean and closing up. Let them go today; let McCorkle look at them tonight.

If he was back tonight. If Frank Pace wasn't quite as fast as all that.

And once Pace was down—*if* he was down— what then? Get close to Akins and kill a marshal? Because Akins would force a fight sure as God made little green apples. Would have to, as Lane would have to in his place. If the lawman wasn't the law, then there was no law. Just a few days deputying over in Idaho a couple of years before had taught Lane that. The law world was another world, different from the way most people lived. You were stud duck, or you were cat shit. There was no in-between in these hard towns.

It was getting to be difficult to see how he could win out, having taken Dowd's two hundred dollars now for several months. Getting to be time to kill some of Parris's sheep-herder friends; Dowd

117

would be expecting that soon enough. First kill their gunman up from Texas, then start killing them. Running them . . . scaring them off. Slaughtering the woolies.

And now saying he hadn't known from the start what would be asked of him as the fight warmed up.

He'd known.

A clever man, seeing nothing but trouble ahead, would point the bay's head toward the mountains and keep going, not go on into town looking to fight a dangerous man with still another dangerous man to fight, even if he won. Not keep hired out to drive off shepherds, either, so Dowd could have his range, and Short-C its range, and the Double-Bar its range, all free of sheep. Damned animals probably didn't do any harm at all, anyway.

A clever man—and God knew Lane had seen the elephant—would turn his horse's head and ride on out. A bit of horse-stealing there, to be sure. But likely Dowd wouldn't send Akins after him for it, not if Lane sent Dowd back the horse's price-and-a-half.

A bit of horse-stealing that way. A bit of horse sense, too. Holliday would have called it horse sense, for sure. He'd never hired his gun in his life.

Wouldn't think as much of Lane now as he had of a wild young man named Buckskin Frank Leslie. Holliday'd liked that young man considerable. But then, Holliday would have probably liked Frank Pace, too, though as a rule he'd no use for Texicans. That skinny, ugly little man had

118

liked any wild one who'd come up to him square, not on the swagger and not scared, either. Pace was likely of that sort. Shot it out with Allison—that handsome, tragic man, with his drunken murders and foul mouth.

Lane remembered the boy Allison had been . . . his short time in Texas so long ago . . . a bank robbery they'd tried out. He and Allison, too young to be scared of Rurales or the Devil staggering out of that Mexican bank laughing so hard they couldn't mount to ride away.

Oh, the great guns. Come to so sad, pinched finishes, most of them. Hardin rotting in the penitentiary. Longley dead. Earp selling real estate in California, for God's sake! Jim Ringgold murdered, shot in the back of the head and left underneath a pinon pine, a book of Greek poetry in his hand.

There was a fight that would have been a fight, if Holliday and Ringgold had gone at it in Tombstone that day. That one would have dried the cows up for sure.

Allison, drunk and fallen out of a farm wagon! Broke his fool neck. That odd little drover, Bonney, dead now in New Mexico, he'd heard. The Hole-in-the-Wall people. Curry, a more than fair shot, he'd heard. And Harry Tracy, a dangerous man. But the rest of them nothing but thieves—opening people's safes, and that sort of thing.

The Thompsons, both gone. Ben, with the fool Jack Omohundro, shot to rags in a variety theatre. Silly damn way to die . . .

It occurred to Lane, as he rode across the bright,

shallow flood of the Little Chicken, that most of the men he'd known well were dead.

Down into the long field that turned to a track and then into the road into Grover, the bay, sweating from the pace, shied at a cloud shadow, and took advantage of that movement to turn its head to bite at Lane's leg.

They were new boots—or almost new. Lane had had Mister Cherry in Grover make them for him. He wasn't about to let the bay gnaw them up. Lane kicked the horse lightly on the nose, and the bay snorted and squealed, made to buck, and then changed its mind.

Lane spurred the beast, and Roscoe grunted and settled down to a loose, steady, rattling run more like a dog's gallop than a proper horse's, but ground-eating, and fine-bottomed. Lane sat the saddle high, though usually he liked to sink down into it like any long-day drover. Do that sort of riding on Roscoe, and the sharp-boned bay would shake some blood into your pee on a long enough go.

On the other hand, what if he were to stay out of the whole bowl of soup? Surely, and soon enough, Pace and Akins would have to find their fight. Akins had been careful not to pick a side—sheep or steer. But his girl ran woolies, and on the trot or not, Marcia Porter seemed to Lane the sort of girl to fairly well neck-rein a man. Even, and maybe especially, a half-sissy like the fierce young marshal.

Lane had seen Porter twice and had from that

first time found her a special twist, though he hadn't taken her upstairs. As a mack, though retired from that strenuous trade for many years, Lane had seen the signs of oddness and secrets on her. A thinking sort of girl—either ashamed or proud of whoring, depending on her mood. A high-strung girl, worth a deal of money to those men who'd enjoy abusing her, or to others, who appreciated a complicated thing.

But not restful.

Lane had wanted a restful girl that night, and had taken a fat brunette with pretty ears. He had, and had not, gotten his rest.

If, now, he were to butt out, let Pace kill a cowman or two, there would surely be cries in Grover for their marshal to earn his bread—all the sharper, if their marshal's popsie stood with Pace on the sheepmen's side.

To keep his badge, Akins would have to face the Texan, and fight him.

And win?

Lane thought—*felt*—not.

He'd never met Frank Pace, but he knew he was an older man than the marshal, of greater reputation—of more murderous reputation. Lane had a feeling about the Texan. That he was a dire fellow in a fight.

Akins was no creamed puff, no piece of pastry at all, but a hard-case, and experienced. But he was young, and had had Segrue to daddy him along—and was a lawman. Pace labored under no such disadvantages.

Pace would kill the marshal certain sure, unless

he tried it at a distance; down a street, or at a corral or feed-lot. Then, Akins' fine aim might make the difference.

Lane thought not.

And, if not, then Lane would have to face Frank Pace, now or later.

Better now than worrying about it. And no knife work, please. Lane's days for wrestling and knife work were done, he thought. Shooting would have to be the way, and better so—and damned if that Texan wouldn't have to be faster than spit off a red-hot stove to stay alive, win or lose.

So you hope, boastful, scared, man. Years too old to be fighting. Scared for sure. But the Bisley Colt's is frightened of nothing.

Up in the mountains, Akins had seen him rolling in the grass, wrestling for his life with a Kiowa buck that Akins could have broken with his hands. Akins had seen him, kicked, cut and beat—had seen him struggle just in time to stab the Indian in the back.

Akins had seen a man, not old as most people thought it, but too old for his game.

It was shaming, Lane thought, for a man to become more scared of death when he had so much less to lose. An embarrassing thing, like farting at a dinner party, with ladies present. It was too embarrassing to bear, to be afraid of the killing he had so often dealt out. It seemed to him he was being a bad sport.

Lane pulled the sweating bay up to a walk, eased the reins, then let them go. He sat the saddle deep as any drover, resting, enjoying the tree shades the horse was walking under. Should have stopped for a drink in the Chicken . . . Doc, he thought, I'm finally running out of sand. It appeared to him, thinking about it, that each of the men he'd killed —a great number—had taken some of his courage with them when they went. Now was the bottom of the sack—but damned if there wasn't some little grit left, at least.

More, perhaps, than the Texan could chew.

Lane took off his Stetson, and wiped the sweat from his face with his jacket sleeve. Then he reached down and eased the Bisley in its holster, something he had never used to do, clucked to the tired bay, and rode down the track into Grover.

SIX

PACE STUFFED a clean pair of socks, long underwear, a clean shirt, and a small-print leather-backed copy of "Our American Cousins" into his saddle-bags. He considered a moment, then added a waxed box of cartridges for the Spencer. Not planning for a war . . . but better have them and not need them, than need them and not have them.

Parris had been a surprise, a younger man than Pace had expected, and a by-God genuine go-to-Jesus parson in the bargain. Must have cut across his grain to be hiring a shooter, and he had, in fact, treated Pace with some contempt. A hired hand, and a nasty one—like the fellow that cleaned out your house drain, if you had a facility indoors.

But that had only been an attitude; he'd said nothing out loud to make Pace angry. Only given him a cool look, up and down, a flicker of a glance to Pace's .44, to the bone handle of the big Bowie.

Then, it had been business. He'd given Pace his one hundred dollars, gold, and offered him a thousand dollars the day no cows at all grazed on the public lands below Faraway creek.

How many grazed there now? And from what ranches?

Parris' thin mouth had thinned some more. Some 20,000 beeves, from four ranches that counted, three that did not count. This was government land, he said, glaring blue-eyed' at Pace, striding up and down. They had their own and all the graze above the Little Chicken. This—*this* land is sheep land.

Parris had a pale wisp of beard, round blue eyes, and thin hands that the veins showed plainly on. It seemed to Pace that Parris was looking for a reason for a fight. He'd seen many like him. People knotted who looked for some fight to cut the knot.

It was hard to see how a reasonable man could love a sheep, unless—as some sheep-herders were rumored to—at the end of a long winter with nothing else.

"Get them off, Mister Pace! Get the damn Babylonians off!"

Parris' own herd—or flock, or whatever— grazed on stony ground, the south face of Old Man mountain. Parris had beckoned Pace to the hotel room window, and pointed the mountain out.

"Two thousand Southdowns—Southdowns! And they are locked up on the worst pasturage in the county." He'd ground his teeth. "Does any man, by God, imagine that I and my friends will stand for it?" . . . And more and more of that sort of thing.

It appeared to Pace that this Yankee had seen too many plays acted in theaters, or fancied himself a John Brown sort of fellow, but about sheep and steers rather than niggers. True enough, some in Texas, who didn't know him personally, might think Pace himself come something down to fight for sheep-men. Those who thought that didn't know him personally.

"I'll take another two hundred and fifty dollars," Pace had said. "There will be expenses, which I do not pay."

The Reverend's mouth had thinned again. "To be deducted from the sum total?" he'd said. And when Pace had nodded, had opened a large coin purse, counted out the eagles, and then noted the amount on a scrap of paper from his pocket.

"I advise you to wipe out a fellow named Breckinridge," the Reverend Parris had said. "He is a beef-raising bully who shot and wounded Monte Isley not two weeks ago. This Breckinridge dog owns Short-C, and beats men with harness leathers when he finds them on his land, innocent and wrong-doing or not." He's paused in talking, to purse his narrow lips, and smack them slightly, as though remembering a meal. "He should certainly be wiped out."

"Fair enough," Frank Pace had said.

It had been a short interview. Pace thought he made the Reverend uncomfortable. Parris had paid him, and thanked him for coming "all this way" and showed him out. They'd met in Parris's room at the Grover House; about an hour meeting, all together, and Parris had not much to add about Harley Akins.

"A decent enough young man," he said, "for one of his sort." Pace hadn't even smiled. "He's kept his skirts clean of alliance with the beef people, I'll say that—thought I can't approve the probable

126

cause." By which Pace took him to mean Akins' being sweet on a sheep-owning whore. "He's done his job well enough here in the town. The rougher sort steer well clear of young Mister Akins." Pace imagined they did.

"As to the ranchers . . .well, you have already had an effect, in dealing as you did with those two drovers. And Mathew Dowd—one of the worst of them, a blood-sucker of the first order—had hired some scar-faced old rounder, I understand, who carries a revolver to threaten people with."

Pace had asked this man's name.

"Lane," Parris had said. "He calls himself, dubiously enough, 'Fenton Lane.'"

Not much in the way of opposition, then—except Akins, who had apparently spent the last day and night off chasing those raggedy-assed Kiowas. For whatever reason, either because he hadn't yet seen the girl, or because she'd lied well enough about that cut, Akins had not come looking Pace up. Pace doubted Akins was shy.

Still, it was as well not to start a job of work by killing a marshal even if it should prove necessary after.

Pace knotted the tie-down on the saddle-bags, swung them up over his shoulder, and picked up the folded map Parris had given him. Parris might be no great shakes as a man of God, but he was a fine hand at map-making. Every track and stream around Grover, every ranch boundary and headquarters house was laid down there neat as in a schoolbook. Pace stuffed the map in his back pocket, reached into a corner to pick up the

Spencer, went out the door, and closed and locked it behind him.

He took the back staircase down to the kitchen, and a fat woman with a wine stain birthmark handed him the midday he'd ordered fixed—two cold pork sandwiches and an apple, wrapped up in a five-pound flour sack.

He walked out into the back alley, and around the corner to the long hitch rail along the side of the building. The old nigger bellman had brought the dun up from the stable, saddled and ready to ride. Pace saw the horse, grained, rested, and rank, shifting roughly against a lean sweated-out bay tied alongside. Pace loosed the reins, ducked under the rail, and shouldered past the bay, noticing a fine old Sharps in the animal's saddle-bucket, then swung his saddle-bags across the dun's rump, tying them fast to the cantle. He strung the lunch sack over the saddle horn and slid the Spencer down into its sheath. Then he checked the cinch—kneed the wind out of the dun, and tightened it—and climbed aboard.

He made, as always, an odd figure, even on so tall a horse. "Like that ape, Abe Lincoln, on a donkey," a friend had once said. Pace reined the dun back out of the horse-line, turned and spurred it, and rode down Main Street at an easy lope, threading through the slower traffic and paying no heed to a drayman's yelling when he cut him close.

In five minutes he was in mountain forest, heading south.

He rode due south for a good while, galloping

128

the rank out of the dun in two long runs, and then drew up in the shelter of an alder grove, took out the Spencer, and sat waiting, quiet on a quiet horse, to see if anyone had followed him out. He thought that Harley Akins might not be too busy to inquire about him, after all, considering the two dead drovers . . . and the whore, Marcia Porter.

Pace thought that he wouldn't have let all that go by, not without some inquiry. Would never believe, for a start, that that girl had broken a glass or whatever and been lightly cut by some piece, flying. Wouldn't believe that and didn't believe Harley Akins would, either.

That had all been—not what he'd intended. Perhaps when he saw the girl again—not to roger her, just to visit—she would think better of him, realize he'd not schemed to take advantage of her profession.

He wondered if the girl cared for reading.

It was possible, too, that the regulator the cattlemen had hired—an older man with a scarred face, Parris had said—might come nosing after. Have to do something about those two drovers, after all, at least make a show of doing something about them.

Not likely to be much trouble there.

Pace sat back in the saddle, easing himself, the Spencer balanced across his saddle bow. Would be coming on to noon now. The bright high-country sunlight streamed through the light green alder leaves all around him, glowing like lime-light. Pace reached down to cover a deerfly biting at the dun's neck, and slowly crushed it, not wanting the noise of a slap.

He sat waiting there for some time listening for hoofbeats coming down the trail. Waiting for the dull thud of them through the ground. Or silence from the birds.

After some time, when he was certain he'd waited long enough, sure that anyone following would have come down by now, he settled himself to wait a little longer. Impatience didn't do. He'd learned that a long time ago.

Pace was some upset with Charles Dickens. It gave him something to think about while he waited and listened.

He didn't of course, blame Dickens for not caring for Yankee hospitality—Yankee homes and Yankee coaches, and Yankee inns. Those people had never, as far as Pace knew, known how to treat a guest. It had been the author's misfortune never to have really known the South, let alone Texas. There, at least, he would have had no cause to complain about rudeness, or unkindness, however simple the welcome he'd been afforded.

Those people had had the greatest writer alive— who'd *ever* lived, as Pace thought, come visit and had treated him roughly and given him bad food.

Still, given all of that, it was hard to acquit the writer of some prejudice. It had made Pace uncomfortable to read his japes against Americans, even the Yankees. For with the exception of Dickens, all the civilized world knew what the British were, and what the Americans had suffered under them. The only Northerners that Pace could honor at all were those men who'd fought the British, and he doubted if any of those men's sons and grandsons had been among the people who'd come down to fight the Confederacy. The Yankees had had their decent men, too.

Pace had regretted and continued to regret that he'd been too young for that war.

Say what you will, though, "Our American Cousins" had been mighty rough on all Americans, and made them seem uncivilized. It was not a fair book—at least as far as Pace had read— and it had been a disappointment to him; that a large-minded man, the author of "David Copperfield," should have proved small-minded about this single matter. Of course, the man wasn't in good health. Pace had read that in the *Houston Chronicle* last year. " . . .*English author in ill health.*"

That would explain a good deal: a great man in ill health was no great man at all.

He'd finish the book, though. Mister Dickens was always worth reading, agree with him or not. Pace had written to Dickens once, but had received no reply.

By early afternoon, he was, taking Parris's map as accurate, on Short-C land. He'd had to take the dun down into a creek bed once, to avoid having to fight three drovers riding by. They hadn't seen him.

The difficulty in things like this was to get to the owners without brushing the hired hands. No use shooting cowboys if he could help it. Any skilled man could kill a drover, and any rancher hire new

131

ones. No doubt the ranch that had hired those two brothers he'd shot would soon have their like hired on. Even drovers could be dangerous, though, if there were enough of them, and they came at a man all together—but Pace had heard of few instances of it, when they faced a prime gun.

He'd stayed down by the run until the pokers had ridden on, then put the dun at the south bank and up into high grass at a steady canter.

There might be luck enough to find Breckinridge at the headquarters house and kill him cold. A squat fellow, Parris had said, with Dutch-yellow hair and bowed legs. "You'll know him by his boots," Parris had said. "The brute wears fine-figured boots with lacing along the sides."

Pace wouldn't depend on luck that fine. If the fellow wasn't there and shootable today, why, he'd probably be so tomorrow. Working ranchers had their rounds and chores and herding they must oversee. So if not today or tomorrow, Pace would find the fellow out soon enough.

Could, of course, have waited for him to come to town, then called him out to draw. But Harley Akins was a problem there. What the marshal might let pass out in the country, he would not let pass in town.

Pace had killed professionals, of course. But the work was harder with that sort and no one paid for it.

The map showed Short-C headquarters seven miles past that run dead on a line with a jagged snow-peak twenty miles further on. Pace wasn't

sure he liked the mountains over there. Too damn
big.

Short-C was a busy ranch. A money-making
operation, to Pace's eyes. Headquarters was no
lone log house; it was half a dozen buildings—
stone walled buildings, some of them—and a
bustle of drovers, wranglers, laborers, and smiths.

A money-making operation for sure. It was sad,
in a way, that Breckinridge had put such years of
effort into building this ranch up only to come to
his end so suddenly.

Pace had tied the dun the other side of a barb-
wire fence, the fence-line fronted by long thickets
of berry bushes. Pace had never seen such country
for berry bushes, and thorny ones, at that. People
said that Texas country was hard on a horse, but
this mountain scrub had clawed the dun's legs
bloody. The berries looked good to eat, and Pace
had seen birds at them, but he didn't choose to
take a fool chance with fruit he didn't know, to
lose a day or two lying under a tree with a gripped
gut. Could be blueberries, wild blueberries. Could
be poison, too.

He hefted the Spencer, kicked through the
brambles, and climbed down into a runoff ditch
reaching to a distant shed. A grainstore, it looked
like, for winter feed. The runoff ditch was a stroke
of luck. No Indian trouble up here for a long time,
that fool bunch of Kiowa aside, for these people to
leave such a concealing approach. A few years of
Comanche trouble would have damn sure taught

them better.

He moved quickly along the ditch, lifted the slack triangle of his bandanna to cover his face up to his eyes. People would know, soon enough. They would be almost certain; ninety percent certain; certain sure. But they wouldn't be able to say they'd seen his face.

No one saw him in the ditch.

He went up the steps to the grain store—well built, he saw, high on fieldstone supports, and tin tacked on all 'round to keep out varmints. Northern kind of building.

He went through the store's narrow, tin-sheathed door, and swung it shut behind him. Dark inside, and hot, the darkness cut by narrow blades of sunlight from ventilation slits up in the loft. Bins on either side of a narrow aisle were heaped with wheat—and this early in the season. Short growing time up in these mountains, but these people took advantage of it.

Pace climbed a short ladder into the loft. It was empty except for a heap of grain sacks in a corner, and clouds of dust bits smoking where the sun shone in.

He walked around the loft, peering out through each horizontal ventilation slit as he came to it.

Too far to the main house. A three-hundred-yard shot, and too far for the Spencer. Needed that fine Sharps he'd seen in that bay's boot . . .

Too far to the main house but nicely near to the corrals, and some shed that must be the smithy.

A fair enough hide to wait in. Until dark. Then

he might get lucky up closer to the house, kill the fellow while he was eating his supper . . .

Pace tugged the bandanna down from his nose and mouth. A man might damn near smother in this sort of place. Slowly, stepping light, he walked the circumference of the loft, stopping at each opening to watch the men coming and going outside. It certainly was a busy ranch. Pace didn't blame the man for not wanting to share his range with sheep. Pace wouldn't have cared to, either, had such a fine property been his.

Certainly not.

Two hours and a bit by Pace's silver-backed watch after he'd come into the storehouse—a quiet two hours and some—Pace heard a man shouting outside opposite to where he was standing, peering out at a wrangler buck-hobbling a roan mare. Pace crossed the loft fast; the shouting voices had "Boss" in it.

He got to the nearest ventilation slit, looked through, and saw a man who had to be Breckinridge—yellow hair, bowlegs, boots and all—plowing through the stable yard dust cursing a streak. Breckinridge was older than Pace had thought he'd be from what Parris had told him. Years of work and weather had sliced deep lines into his face. The Dutch-yellow hair, seen closer, was more grey than yellow.

Breckinridge looked to be a tough cob, and, like the other men in the yard except for the laborers— and the wranglers, who feared hurting themselves falling on them—carried a revolver at his belt.

The fuss appeared to concern a pile of fieldstone the laborers had left heaped alongside the corral. From the words Pace caught, it seemed Breckinridge was worried one of the remuda would break a leg in those stones. In any case, the rancher chested up to one of the workmen and commenced to chew a long strip off of him.

He presented a perfect shot—right side, at a range of one hundred yards, give or take a few feet.

Pace felt that he had to pee. He often felt that before he killed a man but when at times he'd been able to pause to take a piss then, he'd found he hadn't the need after all.

Pace stood a little back from the ventilation slit, cocked the Spencer and raised it for a fine bead . . .

Then he heard the door downstairs swing open and slam shut.

Footsteps.

Monte Irvine had been a heller in his youth—a skinny, root-tough little drover, quick with his fists and boots in any kind of fight. He'd cowboy'd through the early years, the best years when Goodnight and Loving, Chisholm and the others were pioneering the cattle trails and the cattle business.

Monte had worked for Chisholm for three years, had ridden the great early drives, once with a fresh-broke arm in a hasty sling. He'd circled stampede leaders, and fought border ruffians and Pawnees and loved it all.

Monte, seventy-four years old now, could remember when American drovers and Texicans were still learning the ropes from vaqueros along the Bravo.

Monte had worked and ridden in the sunshine of the cattle trade. He'd heard of the fine days of mountain beaver trapping, as all drovers had, but had never been able to imagine a better life than the one he had—wild, free-running (at least before the wire came in) and with friends beside him. Not lonely as the old mountain men had had to live.

So he'd worked his life out, riding through the seasons, roping, chasing strays, branding and later, fixing fence.

The years had fled past him like so many days, and he'd waked one morning to find that he'd become old.

The golden life was past. The old bone-breaks, the chills of wet snow camps, the endless days and nights riding . . . riding, all came back upon him in his age, and bent and twisted him like a wire sample in a drummer's case. Chores were what he was good enough for now. Watering, sweeping and swamping, keeping the chickens. All the sunny fine years had come down to that. Monte never had been much for complaining—it was a habit he'd never fallen into. He took the cowhands' ragging and did his work as best he could. Sometimes, in his dreams, he grew young again overnight, and in that dream would walk out of the bunk-house in the morning as a strong, hard-faced boy with buckboard springs for legs—and would then, by God, show the ragging drovers how the young man hidden in the old man could cowboy.

He'd dreamed that dream just a night or so ago and was thinking about it when he went into the grain store for a sack of feed. Mrs. Dowd fancied Barred Rocks for sitting hens, not caring, or knowing, likely, that those big hens ate up more feed than they laid in eggs. "I care for the taste of those eggs," she'd said. "Monte, you keep those hens healthy, now."

Any other chickens would have done better yard-scratching; not the Barred Rocks. A round pound of feed every day was what those damn feather dusters required. A pound! And not a bird more than twenty in the flock.

Foolishness. Monte ascribed it to the Breckinridges' having come from Utah.

He pushed open the tin-sheathed door, a feed sack in his hand, and limped over to the near left bin. Fine cracked corn. For chickens! The Irvines had raised seven children on cornmeal mush in Uvalde county in the years before the war. Did his old Mam know in her grave he was feeding chickens fine cracked corn, she's spin like a store-bought whip-top!

Monte had gotten to the bin and shaken the feed sack open to ladle a scoop or two into it, when he heard a noise, looked up—and saw the damndest thing.

A giant man jumped down from the loft trap without touching the ladder—right down out of the darkness—and landed on the store house floor with hardly a sound. Monte thought it was a man when he first saw it, but then it came at him with a great big knife in its hand, and he saw its face and thought that the Devil had come to get him. It had grey eyes, soft as a woman's . . .

Pace reached the old man and struck at him with the Bowie as he stood staring, toothless mouth hanging open, in the sunlight falling from the half closed door.

Somehow, the old man got a hand up to ward, and the broad, heavy knife blade chopped through the thin wrist and left the hand to dangle by a tendon.

Pace struck him again, and drove the blade down into the old man's head with the sound of opening a summer melon.

The old fellow fell, kicking an odd, rapid heel-drumming kick as if he were running into death as fast as he could, and Pace put his boot on him to hold him still while he wrenched the Bowie free.

Then Pace spun about—leaped to the loft ladder and up it as quick as a cat, crossed the loft floor to pick the Spencer up from where he'd gently set it down and, leaning to the ventilation slit, saw Breckinridge still standing, rating the workman.

He'd turned, just a little, to the right, to point over at the stone pile. But not enough to spoil the shot.

Luck.

Pace raised the Spencer, took his bead and shot the man into the pit of his right arm.

A killing shot.

Pace didn't wait to see the rancher fall. He turned in a swirl of powder smoke, the blast of the shot still echoing in his ears, tugged the bandanna up to cover his face, and jumped back down the loft trap.

He hit the floor below running, cleared the old man's body and was at the door and out of it, down into the drainage ditch, and galloping like a horse for the distant brambles and the barb-wire fence where the dun was tied.

He ran as fast as a running colt and felt as fine, the giddy, pleasant feeling he always knew in such circumstances.

Behind him, he heard shouts, men running, and a galloping horse. He wouldn't be able to beat the horse to those brambles.

Pace turned, still running, the rifle balanced in his left hand, and saw a small pinto spurred fast around the grain store corner and lined out on him. A wool-hatted rover was up and whipping, a revolver in his other hand.

Pace jolted to a stop, half turned, drew his .44 and fired. He heard the solid thump as the lead went home, and saw the cowpoker thrown far back along the cantle, his hat flying away.

He pinto kept coming, the dying man aboard, and Pace lit out running again, only yards now from the tethered dun. The pinto ran alongside him for a moment, making a race of it. The pony's flank was washed with bright red.

Then the pinto shied away, and the drover, soaked with blood, rolled off him dead, fell free of the stirrups, and struck the earth with a smack.

Now bullets began to snap and sing past Pace as he ran; two men stood at the grain store, shooting at him with pistols. Pace didn't turn to fire again; he ducked his head, stayed as deep in the ditch as he could, and kept running, his boots pounding the rutted dirt.

The brambles were close. Pace heard hoofbeats again, some distance back. He strained to run even faster—saw the end of the ditch . . . reached it . . . and jumped up into the thorny brush. Bulled his way through it. Put his hand on a fence post and vaulted the wire—tore the dun's reins free—forked, and spurred him—and rode.

He galloped the dun down a narrow pasture, hearing the shouts, the hoofbeats coming behind him, jumped the big horse over a shallow ditch, and drove it, raking hard, up and over the ditch bank.

Rifle fire. Pace heard the rounds cracking past him.

He turned the foaming dun to a stand of trees lying left along a meadow—a foaling pasture, by the mares and young standing, ears up, to watch him thunder past. The dun ran breasting into the first growth of saplings, vines, brush then tried to slow. But Pace struck him with the spurs again, and the dun stretched out into a swerving run through undergrowth and larger and larger trees.

They burst out into more pasture, and Pace heard the chase soften, confused, behind him, as the drovers milled in the woods, finding their way.

He did not let the dun slack off, but booted him on in a lunging gallop, sailing down a steep creek-cut slope—a sudden *splash-splash* as they struck the narrow stream—and driving, heaving up the other side, crashing through a line of brush.

Pace turned the laboring horse to the left again,

141

and drove him running along the creek line into the timber and pulled him down to a trot, reining him through a maze of lodge-pole, alder, and spruce.

After a while, at a walk.

Two hours later, on the road into Grover, Pace sat his weary horse, singing. He sang the "Great Blue Hen," and then he leaned back in the saddle, hummed a bit, and sang "Green Grow The Rushes, Oh." He sang it at the top of his voice, all the verses.

SEVEN

LANE HAD spent an hour sitting in the front lobby of the Grover House, sitting back at his ease in one of the armchairs usually occupied by a fat drummer. He'd smoked a Havana cheroot while he waited.

No Frank Pace. The desk clerk, a pleasant young man named Harris, hadn't seen Pace go in or out since the night before.

After the hour, Lane had gone up to the Texan's room.

"No trouble, now—is there going to be trouble, Mister Lane?" Harris, an Englishman, was a good desk clerk—had clerked in San Francisco for awhile.

Lane didn't lie to him.

"Maybe," he said.

"Hell's bells," Haris said, "This is the nicest place in town! The buyers won't stand for shooting, Mister Lane. They'll make the ranchers sweat."

"It can't be avoided," Lane said, "not for long."

"Maybe Akins will run him out," Harris said. "I'll tell you this; he looks to be a fierce one. Bad as he's been made out, as far as I can tell." Harris had been around some.

Then, Lane had gone upstairs.

That short climb had cost him a little. It had taken a bit and then some to knock on Frank Pace's door. Lane stood a little to the left side, waiting.

Frank Pace hadn't been there.

Feeling a fool, and ashamed to be relieved at the Texan's being gone, Lane went down to Pierce's Livery, and found that Pace had had his horse called for that morning.

The fellow was loose.

Lane had no doubt the Texan had gone scouting at the least—and killing, if there was the opportunity for it. Pace wouldn't be the sort to waste time at a job like this.

No use hound-chasing the man all over the country and be just missing him at every turn. Dowd was paying first of all for a guard on Broken Iron. Lane would have to get back out to the ranch, make damn sure Pace hadn't decided to start his murders with Dowd's spread.

It seemed to Lane that two hundred dollars a month was a fair wage after all. Might not be enough, in fact.

And since war it seemed to be, war it would be.

Parris held his herd on the south flank of the Old Man. It would be the long way round, but an opportunity to give the sheep people a lesson of their own and to give the Texan something to think about, as well.

A *regulator*. How Holliday would have laughed at it all.

Lane walked back up the alley from Pierce's to

where he'd left the bay tethered alongside the Grover House rail. As he rounded the corner, he saw Harley Akins standing by the bay. Akins saw him at the same time, and stood waiting for him.

Lane paid attention to how the marshal was standing, how he held his shoulders. It didn't look like trouble—not serious trouble.

"What are you doing in town?" Akins said to him. His voice was easy as ever, but his eyes looked odd, something of a yellow light in the brown.

Lane saw no reason to lie to him.

"I intended to have a talk with this Texan, Pace, that's come to town. I believe he's here to push some for the sheep raisers."

Akins turned his big head, as a young bull would, to look off down the street. "That may be your business, out in the range . . . on Broken Iron land," he said, still looking off down the street. "It *isn't* your business, here in town. It's my business."

Hard to argue with that. For now.

Akins looked straight at him. "The Texan has done nothing in town I know of. Until he does, he can come and go like any other man." It occured to Lane that Akins had taken his side at last. Likely the sheep-men's side, to let Pace run free in Grover. The little whore, Marcia, had turned him up sweet, after all.

"That go for me as well?"

"You're a Broken Iron man," Akins said. "You stay on out there for a while."

"Don't come into town?"

"Don't come into town," Akins said. "I won't have a shooting gallery here."

May as well ask it.

"And if I do?"

There was no change in Akins' face. "If you do, if you come in again until I say you can, I'll have to jail you for it—or kill you, if you resist."

No threat to any of it—more a serious promise.

"My, my," Lane said. "It appears us Indian-fighters might fall out."

Akins stared at him with no expression at all, but Lane knew he was thinking of the boy and knew Lane was, too. A man and woman walked past them, going on into the hotel. The man had glanced at them when he'd walked by, noticed something about the way they were talking, the way they were standing.

And for sure, Lane would never have a better chance at Akins than right now. The marshal was no more than two feet from him—up close, for sure. And the chance was there as well to call him for what he'd done to that Kiowa boy.

Now—or maybe never.

Akins stood, bulky and still, staring at him.

And Lane decided against it. He hadn't reason enough to kill the young man, presuming he could get it done if he tried. Not reason enough to be killing a town marshal just because he'd been posted out of town. It was common sense. Common sense, to back down.

Or something else.

"Now," Lane said, "I'll certainly try and avoid that kind of trouble with you, Marshal. If I can."

Akins said nothing, just stood still, and watched Lane untether the bay and climb up into the saddle—watched him back the animal away from the rail, turn it, and ride off down the street.

Lane found, as he rode out, that his right hand had made a fist, striking softly against the saddle-bow. A long time to live, to be so shamed. He felt his face flush like a girl's. Not that it hadn't been the best thing to have done; to have fought the marshal would have been a fool's act just now. But . . . his fist knocked against the saddle-bow as regular as any steam engine's working. But only a few years ago, only a few damn years ago . . .

Would have only laughed, when that hard-case pup had posted him, laughed and told him to come on. Shot the marshal's buttons off. Tried that ten years ago, that would have been what happened. Would have shot that boy-lover's buttons right off him.

Just a few god-damned years.

Buckskin Frank Leslie . . . By God, there was a laugh!

Lane rode out of Grover on the western road, then turned the bay onto a track leading south-west. Run out of town like a damn dog, he thought, and had to smile. You fool. A man grown and past his prime at that caught short playing wild kid's games. Hell, I have never grown full up; that's my trouble. Used my revolver to play the heller, long past the time to turn it in.

He thought of himself, riding out of town, grey-haired, red-faced as any picked-on schoolyard lad, and laughed out loud. Older and scared—or older and wiser. Or older, scared *and* wiser, more likely.

It seemed to have become natural to him—not to be so sudden and fierce as he wanted to be.

No use getting into the sullens about it.

If he had to go into Grover after the Texan, if it proved something he couldn't avoid, then young Harley Akins would have to take his chances. The three of them, after all—himself, Akins, and Frank Pace—had all been in the game for some time. They were being paid, by whoever, to take their chances.

Hell, he'd lived ten men's lives already. Wouldn't do to be too greedy.

By afternoon, he was up on the south slope of the mountain, sitting the sweated-out bay, and watching a herd of sheep through a screen of dwarf willows.

The hard ride had done him good, settled those whim-whams for him.

Lane saw nothing but sheep for the first minutes of watching, then he reached around to pull the little telescope from his saddle bags and used it to glass the woods on the other side of the meadows.

It took him three slow sweeps before he saw it.

A smudge of smoke hanging low in the thick-leaved green. Sycamores, hickories. Somebody over there knew how to build a quiet fire. And, more important, knew it was wise to build a slight fire just now. Knew trouble was likely. Knew, or had heard, of Pace being paid to come in on their side.

Lane tried no odd approach. Having seen the fire, he tucked the little glass away, loosened the big Sharp's in its scabbard, and touched the bay's flanks with his spurs.

He rode out across the wide meadow at an easy lope, riding through the short mountain bunch-grass, so sharply green in the upland air. He rode through sunlight and cloud shadows past scattering sheep, as the thunderheads came marching high over the head of the Old Man. Tilting the brim of his Stetson up, Lane could see the flash and glitter of snow high on the mountain peak.

There was no movement in the woods in front of him.

He loped the bay through the bordering brush and on into the trees, pulled him down to a walk, and let him amble, blowing, getting his wind back. It had been long riding today, from the Iron into Grover, and now this long, long way home.

Lane smelled smoke drifting on a slow breeze, and guided the bay that way. Not a quarter of a mile into the trees, likely, otherwise the camp would be too far from the sheep in case of trouble.

He'd gone along the way for a short time when he heard barking and, in a few moments, a small black and white, shaggy-furred dog came bounding out of the vines, barking and snarling, and making to rush at the bay and bite his legs. The horse paid no heed to him, and the dog redoubled his noise and his rushing, veering away from the bay each time at the last instant, retreating, uttering more threats.

Fine camp guards, dogs. Lane wondered why

they weren't more popular with cattle people. There were usually some hounds or curs kept at the home place but dogs weren't used with the stock at all, except some rare exceptions, pets who helped a family bring in its few head.

Handy at a camp, all the same. There surely would be no surprising these sheep people, even if he'd ridden wide just to do that.

The smoke smell was soon stronger and the small dog more furious. Lane saw the less complicated sunlight of a clearing just ahead, and bent his head as the bay shoved through low-hanging branches, rustling bright green curtains of leaves.

He rode out into the clearing with the dog, enraged, still at his horse's heels. Two men stood beside a patched U.S. Army tent in the midst of a litter of dismounted buckboard parts, fire pits, sheepskins, feed pails, horse blankets, tool boxes, grub boxes, and a splintered medicine crate full of brown linement bottles, blow-fly ointment, and patent baby bottles with black India rubber nipples. Clothes hung on a long line between two trees, and a wash tub full of more sat steaming in the coals of a careful fire.

One of the two men was old, a Mexican with long white mustaches and a dimpled closed eyelid where his left eye had been. He had a rifle in his hands—a trap-door Springfield with a sawed-short barrel.

The other man was younger and looked like the old man's son. He had a slight mustache, nothing so fine as the old man's, and bright black eyes like a bird's. He was holding a single-barrel shotgun pointed at Lane's head, and seemed a quick tempered sort of fellow.

"Good day," Lane said in somewhat rusty border Spanish. *"Forgive me entering your camp uninvited, but unfortunately I must discuss business with you. A shame on this most beautiful day which God has given us."*

Lane thought he'd done that rather well; it had been years and then some since he'd ridden out of Old Mexico, but neither of the shepherds seemed to think much of it.

"Get out," the younger man said, in more than passable English.

His father cocked the Springfield.

"Not before we talk our business," Lane said, sitting easy on the bay, and keeping his hand away from the Bisley Colt's.

There was what Holliday would have called a pregnant pause.

But they didn't make to shoot.

Lane reflected, not for the first time, on how helpless most people were, facing someone experienced in violence. It was difficult for most men to simply shoot another man down without there having been an argument, at least, or a display of temper.

These Mexicans should have shot him as he came riding out of the woods, still ducking branches—or tried to, at any event. Now, aimed weapons or not, they'd lost their chance.

"Do you know who I am?" he said. More than one answer to that, as it happened.

"Yes," the younger Mexican said, over the

barrel of the shotgun. "You're the *pistolero* who rides for Dowd."

A fair enough answer.

"Yes," Lane said. "I am. And my business here is to make sheep-running a difficult thing to do." They watched him, and listened and they didn't shoot. "I am going to burn your camp," Lane said. "I would rather not have to kill you to do it—"

He was looking at the old man's face as he said it, saw his mouth suddenly open a little in astonishment, and threw himself hard to the side of his saddle.

The load of shot snatched his Stetson off and shredded it like hotel lettuce, and the bay whinnied and spun like a top. Lane couldn't quite get back up in the saddle—he was damn near out of it and onto the ground as the horse whirled, half bucking, and Lane saw the young man running at him with the empty shotgun swinging to beat out his brains.

Lane stopped fighting; let the horse toss and whirl him; forced his hand down to the Bisley's butt—pulled the weapon—and, as the bay crow-hopped hard to the left, shot the young Mexican through his shoulder.

Then Lane reached with his left hand, got he reins as they flew, and did his damndest to yank the bay's teeth out. The dog was yelling and snapping away as the bay shuddered and sidled to a stand.

Hanging off the horse's side like a railroad tagger catching a stockyard freight, Lane looked for the old man and saw him with his son, trying to

152

hold him up. The young man was staggering, bleeding hard. The old man had left the Springfield in the grass.

Lane lunged up once, missed, and lunged up again, caught hold of the horn and hauled himself back up into the saddle. The wrenching had opened the cuts down Lane's side, and he was angry enough at the bay to shoot the fool between the ears—wouldn't mind putting that damn sheep dog away, either!

The Stetson was a dead loss. Lane could see it down in the dirt, shot to rags. A twenty dollar hat!

"You there!" he said, and not in Spanish, either. "Old man, you get me the best hat you have in camp!"

The old man did not argue. He helped his son sit down. The young man's face was the color of spoiling milk. The bullet looked to have broken his shoulder and might bleed him out to death if it kept leaking. Still and all it had been a considerable shot. From a wheeling horse, too. Some sort of stuff in the old fart yet.

The old man came hustling out of their tent with a fancy-stitched old *sombrero* with a one-foot brim curled up three inches around the edges. The crown was a foot high, easy.

"Give me that hat," Lane said, and the old man came over and handed it up. Lane tried it on, and it was a little tight, but he jammed it on anyway.

"Now go help your boy. Wrap that bullet hole hard, or you'll lose him." The old man nodded. He was weeping, scared of losing his son. "Wrap it hard."

153

Lane stepped down off the bay, dropped the reins and waited to see if the brute would stand, then walked over to their laundry fire and bent and picked out a burning brand. He went to their tent, and, after two tries, set it on fire. When it was burning well, he picked up all their sheep gear, box by box, and threw it into the flames. He threw in everything, even their clothes off the line, and he dumped their wash tub over into the coals and ashes of the fire pit. Then he picked up the wheels and side boards of their buckboard—taken down for greasing, he supposed—and threw them one by one into the burning tent.

When Lane glanced at the Mexicans, he saw that the old man had gotten his son's shirt off, twisted the bloody cloth into a bandage, and had tied it tight enough under the young man's armpit and over his shoulder to stop the worst of the bleeding. The young Mexican looked sick as a horse—he had the dull, dreaming look that Lane had seen in many badly injured men. The bone in the shoulder was broken for sure.

Lane found their horse—a scrub, just fit for pulling their buckboard—and started to loose it and set it running. Then he thought of the hurt man. If he couldn't ride out, he wouldn't get out. Lane left the horse alone, and looked 'round the camp once more for something to burn. But he'd used it all up.

The fire smoke was smelling pretty good now. The bacon in their grub box must be cooking.

He went back to the bay—for a wonder, the sidling plug had stayed put—and mounted, not without a sharp reminder from the cuts down his side.

He beckoned the old man to him.

"Old one," he said in Spanish. *"I ask you to spare me the necessity of killing one who might have been my father. Leave this country as soon as your boy can travel, and never come back."*

The old man only nodded, but his son was feeling strong enough to have something to say.

"If my brother were here, you *cabron*, he would have killed you!"

Lane smiled. *"Your other son,"* he said to the old man, *"he is a fierce one? A pistolero?"*

"My son, Euselbio, was a thief, a bandit. Now he is a sergeant with the Rurales."

Lane nodded. *"He sounds a dangerous man. But it is a sad truth that dangerous men are usually present when they are not wanted and often absent wen they are."*

He turned the bay, and spurred him across the clearing. *"Go with God, old one!"* The dog barked him out of camp.

Lane rode up the long meadow bordering the woods, scattering sheep to either side of the loping bay. Just like one of Ned Buntline's heroes . . . "Go with God." Not bad doings, altogether. The young Mex ought to recover, though maybe with a stiff shoulder. The scrub was enough horse to get them back to Parris's, the young man riding, the old man walking lead. Interesting to see how Pace would take the news—likely he'd already done some damage, already possibly killed someone.

Now he wouldn't have to worry about getting up the nerve to find the Texan. Pace would come after him, and pronto.

Probably should have killed a bunch of sheep today. That was the usual thing to do—shoot up some of the opposition's stock. But it hadn't ever made sense to do that to Lane. The poor dumb brutes had nothing to do with the trouble—no use taking the trouble out on them. Quite a number of men, he'd found, deserved killing, one way or another. Never had found an animal that did unless it was a lobo, or stock-killer.

The bay was starting to labor, and Lane pulled him down to a walk. He'd be glad to get the stout pinto under him again; a horse that couldn't stand gunfire was no use to him at all. A positive danger, in fact. If that had been Harley Akins or Frank Pace facing him in that clearing, the bay would have gotten him killed first shot loosed.

The cloud shadows were longer now, drifting more slowly over the rising grasslands, the dark green tree-lines running the sides of the Old Man. He'd cut across the east ridge to Broken Iron land, be back at the bunk-house before dark—and, please the lord, not find that Pace had stolen a march on him by hitting the Iron his first day out fighting. Dowd wouldn't care how many Mexicans Lane had shot up, then.

It was hot, riding. Lane reached up to tug the *sombrero* off his head. Damn thing was too tight, giving him a headache. Have to go to Pabst's in Grover, buy himself a new hat. Been thinking about a different color, maybe a fine light grey

Stetson, with one of those new low crowns like Californians wore . . . He rode slowly along, fanning himself with the *sombrero*—more use as a fan, than a hat. Felt better, now that he'd done some work. His kind of work. Been thinking about it too much. Shooting didn't bear too much thinking on. It was something you could do or something you couldn't.

So far, it was still something he could do. When it wasn't, Lane thought, he'd just be an old range bum—a pickup man, a swamper. Or he'd be dead.

Day this pretty, it didn't seem to matter. He saw a small shadow race across the grass, looked up, shading his eyes with his hand, and saw a hawk—a red-tail it looked—sailing past up high. Veering, sliding sideways with the wind as it flew. The hawk flew right under the sun as Lane watched, was silhouetted against the blaze of light for an instant, then flew out into the blue-white of the mountain sky.

Pretty day. New summer flowers under the bay's hooves. Smell of horse sweat and leather, smell of gunpowder, too, from the shooting. His side was troubling him a little, the cuts opened from all that buckerooing when the bay acted up. Lane pulled the horse up, and swung down to stand in the thick bunch grass. Felt better standing than riding.

He stepped out, leading the bay. Rest the horse —rest his side, too.

The ridge was a climb, and had Lane sweating fine by the time he reached the crest. The wind blew more strongly there, though, streaming up the east slope and combing over the ridge line so strongly you felt you could see it—kind of a thickening, a whitening in the air just over the stone and stunted trees along the crest. Cool air down from the peaks of the hills, the snow fields high on the Old Man. It dried the sweat on Lane's face, molded his clothes to him as he stood with the bay grazing behind him, looking out over Broken Iron. Even through the cool, he felt the high mountain sun stinging his unprotected forehead. Skin there was milk white in contrast to the furniture mahogany of his face where no Stetson had covered it.

Holding the bay's reins looped over his left arm, Lane reached down to the top of his right boot, tugged the Arkansas toothpick free, and sliced a slit through the *sombrero's* band. Shame to ruin a good hat but if the damn thing didn't fit, it didn't fit.

He slid the knife back into its scabbard, and tried the hat. Much better—a lot better. He tipped the wide brim down to shade more of his face.

All of Broken Iron lay beneath him; a long, long, gently rolling stretch of country—a great valley, really, between the true range of the Rockies, and a line of foothills ten miles and more to the east.

Down there, was everything a range man could desire: stands of timber a mile deep and more, hardwood and pine; a full-sized river, the Mazy, and the Little Chicken, to the south end of the land; and grass. Fine rich sea-green mountain grass, sprung up out of limestone rocks and glacier washes. Grass that sprouted stout steers, and steel-boned horses. And all under the shoulders of the mountains, that took the eastward weather and broke it, and spread it like a gentle country quilt over this country.

It was the prettiest that Lane had known.

That this wonderful ranch—wonderful even to a townsman, a smoky-room gambler, a fine-furnished pimp-that-was—wonderful even to him, that all this should belong to a company of Englishmen and Canadians and God knew who else and be major-owned by Mathew Dowd, seemed at once a funny and a nasty thing.

Lane had often wondered at the hunger which led decent men, large-scaled men, full of the love of life, to murder and scheme in order to lay claim to another section, another more distant line and border. This hunger just for more and more dirt and cow-graze, had puzzled him. But the look of Broken Iron from a mountainside went a way toward explaining all that.

For a while, cooling out in the steady wind, he'd watched a small herd of elk drifting down below out of range of even the Sharps, had he felt like making that much noise. The elk were out in the heat of the sun, which was unusual. But they and the big mule deer were often fooled by cloud shadows and storm clouds shading the slopes lower down, took that for evening, and drifted down to graze before night.

The wind was in his face, and the bay's so the first he knew of the horseman was the thudding through the earth.

Lane and the bay turned their heads together to

look back the way they'd come and saw a man riding up toward them, not more than a few hundred yards away.

It was a rider in a hurry flailing at his horse; a very fine horse, Lane noticed, a big grey, looked like a stallion. When he'd seen how the man rode, Lane knew even at that distance that it wasn't Akins and certainly wasn't the Texan.

Whoever, was coming right for him and had, no doubt, been riding after him for an hour or more. No trouble following Lane's track—the bay had trotted out a nice trail through the bunch grass. Careless there. A little too busy congratulating himself on that tricky shot, playing Fancy-Dan with his border Spanish.

Lane climbed up onto the bay and spurred him a few yards back down the ridge toward the horseman, to win a little room to ride in should it come to a fight. Then he reached down and pulled the Sharps out of its bucket.

Better to have it and not need it than need it and not have it.

The rider was closer now, still having at the stallion with a crop. In a terrible hurry for sure. That was quite a horse, pushing on up the ridge as if it were running on level ground. Closer . . . The rider was Reverend James Able Parris.

Lane put the big Sharps back. Parris was a talker—was bound to want to get close enough to talk, or shout or whatever. Handgun range.

Parris looked mad as fire.

Closer . . .

Parris was shouting something, waving his

160

whip. Horse must be something relieved. Lane saw no weapon. The fool must be unarmed. To start the kind of trouble he'd started, and then ride the country unarmed—a troublesome fool.

"Damn you! Damn you!"

Mad as fire.

Parris pulled up before him, the stallion a lather of sweat, prancing, dancing sideways, almost slipping the shouting man off his saddle. Parris hit the animal across the neck with the crop.

"Be *still*, won't you!"

The stallion whinnied and tried to back, but Parris hit it again, and put spurs to it until it quieted, trembling.

"Now, you—" he said, pointing the crop at Lane. "I met—just an hour ago—two of my people, the Orellanas, coming to my home wounded and abused—by *you*, you scar-faced coward!"

The young Reverend's face was red, and as he shouted, Lane saw foam flecking the pale, wispy beard.

Lane held up his hand, and Parris was quiet for a moment.

"I'll pass that personal remark," Lane said. "Now, you listen to me. Any man that comes onto range to do stock business has got to expect some trouble with it. If you can't stand the trouble then get off the open range!" Parris opened his mouth, but Lane rode right over him. "You can't go hiring hoodlums from Texas and not expect some difficulty for your own. Where is your man, and what is *he* doing now?"

Lane had read often of men grinding their teeth

in rage, but he'd never really seen it. He saw it now. Parris seemed convulsed with fury.

He screamed at Lane like a furious woman: "You—you *devil!* It was devils like you that killed my father! You killed him in the Wilderness— devils just like you, full of wealth and fat with evil!"

"You're not in church, you jackass," Lane said, but Parris wasn't listening to him.

"Swollen—oh, *swollen* with evil, like a mighty demon tick that sucks and sucks the poor man's sustenance! Slave-holder! Brute! And *devil!*" He paused to take a breath.

Lane saw that the man took him for an old Johnny Reb; many had. It appeared to him that he was facing a quaint type of New England madman. Righteous unto madness.

He tried to calm the fellow down.

"Now, see here," he said. "That's all bullshit. This is only a matter of grass and stock—and money. You might call me a representative of the cattle interests in a straightforward sort of way. Just so, you've hired a representative of your interests. Now, I suggest you go on home and let us representatives settle the matter. We're being paid to do that."

Lane thought for a moment that Parris had calmed. He'd seemed to listen while Lane was talking. Then, when he finished, Lane saw in Parris's eyes nothing but an odd determination.

Parris raised his riding crop, leaned forward in his saddle, and struck at Lane's face with it, grunting with the effort of the blow.

Lane caught the whip in his left hand. The blow had come with a crack, and numbed him to his elbow.

Then he reached over with his right hand, seized the man's jacket collar, and dragged him half over from his saddle.

"Oh, will you whip me?" Lane said. He let go with his right hand for an instant, drew the Bisley, and, as Parris struggled to regain his balance, hit him once across the face with the revolver and broke his nose, and again as he fell sideways toward the ground and broke his right cheekbone.

Lane leaned far over to strike the man a third time as he fell, to beat in the back of his head but he stopped himself from doing it.

"You fortunate man," Lane said, as Parris fell stretched out into the grass. The stallion backed, reared, and ran, tripping once on a dangling rein.

The bay had stood still for this. Gunfire troubled him, apparently—blows didn't.

Lane sat the saddle, watching Parris down in the grass. After several minutes, Parris came to himself and slowly began to struggle up onto his hands and knees. It took him some doing. While he watched, Lane dug back into his saddle-bags, found a cigar half, took it out and scratched the lucifer on his boot sole to light it.

Parris rested on his hands and knees for some time—appeared unable to stand up, or to want to try. Blood was running from his face in a thin, bright string of red into the grass. Lane had thought the man might have a small pistol concealed about him, perhaps in the skirts of his frock coat, that Lane might have missed, just looking. But it appeared no such thing. Parris made no move for a weapon; perhaps was feeling too poorly.

The thought of a weapon reminded Lane of his own revolver, and he drew the Bisley again, examined the barrel and front sight, and spun the cylinder. He'd seen many fine pieces ruined by striking some fool's hard head.

The Bisley was undamaged, though, and he put it away and sat, one leg cocked up across the saddle bow, puffing on the last of the Grover House cheroot.

Parris made a try to get to his feet, but only got half up, sitting. His arms were shaking.

Parris had not looked up at Lane. Now, he did.

His broken face was the color of clay, except for his mouth and beard. They were running red with blood, and his shirt front was drenched with it.

His eyes held an expression that Lane had seen many times before. There was a satisfied look to them, as if Parris already saw Lane dead and was pleased, in some way, at what Lane had just done to deserve it.

It was a look that had frightened Lane the first few times he'd seen it, more than twenty-five years before.

Now it only made him tired.

"The second blow I hit you," Lane said, "I struck for your horse."

Then he nudged the bay's head around, touched him with the spurs, and trotted him off, over the crest of the ridge, and down the long grassy slope onto Broken Iron.

He was well past the Little Chicken, riding into a considerable sunset, when he saw two Iron drovers, Mixton Evans and Pierce Owen, riding toward him. They had their rifles out, and looked pretty pert.

Mixton rode over to him, and said, "Hi-de-do?" Mix had been up at the north line camp the past two weeks. Then Lane saw Dowd and Mrs. Dowd in their surrey following behind. Lane supposed that Frank Pace had already made a mess, for the Dowds to ride guarded. He hadn't made a mess on Broken Iron, though, or there'd be four guards, not two.

The Dowds had apparently been visiting over at the Chamblees'. Lane had never met Chamblee, who ran a small horse operation—fine Morgan crossbreeds—just over the Mazy. Chamblee, who had no part in the range quarrel, was a gentleman from Philadelphia. His wife, Lane had heard, had a consumption. Likely, they had come west for that reason. Same reason Holliday had, come to that. Probably do just as much good, too. None, poor lady.

"Now, there, Lane!" Dowd pulled up his horses, and beckoned Lane over. "Where in the world have you been, man? Don't you know that Clete Breckinridge is dead?"

So the Texas had gone to Short-C first. Must have a good map, to find his way across strange country so neatly.

"Breckinridge was shot dead with a rifle aimed from his own grain store!" Dowd was bouncing gently up and down on the surrey seat as he talked, considerably excited. Up on the surrey seat, he looked even smaller than usual. Not by any means for the first time, Lane wondered how the little man and his wife accomodated themselves to the difference in size.

Mrs. Dowd sat beside her husband, smiling slightly at his excitement, slowly twirling her parasol, first in one direction, then the other.

She was not a fat woman, but large and big-boned. She had a long white face, a long fine nose with small, curled, elegant nostrils, and a wide, genial, generous mouth. She looked to have large breasts and buttocks, and was quite the favorite subject of discussion among the rougher drovers when Shand couldn't overhear.

Mrs. Dowd—Catherine Dowd—had clever, amused brown eyes, and was almost six inches taller than her husband.

She was from Canada, too, from the city of Vancover on the Pacific ocean. No one on the ranch knew what her parents had been, or what sort of family she came from. But, she was a lady.

Her hair was the color of her eyes, and looked long enough, if let down, for even such a large, tall woman to sit upon, if she chose to try it, sitting in her nightgown at her vanity.

"Only Breckinridge?" Lane said.

"No," Dowd said, stopped in mid-flight. "Pace killed an old chicken keeper and a drover, too."

"Anybody see his face?"

"No," Dowd said, "but it was certainly that Texas savage. Who else could have done that?"

"Had a bandanna over his phiz," Pierce Owen said, throwing in his two cents. It was his only put-in. Dowd gave him a look, and Pierce, abashed, backed his pony and trotted away rifle ready, back on guard.

"And what have you been doing, this busy day, Mister Lane?" Catherine Dowd said.

"Now, let's see . . ." Lane said. "Nothing so fatal as Pace has, I suppose. I wounded a Mex herder, burned a sheep camp and beat James Parris a bit."

"Have you, by God?" Dowd bounced up and down on the surrey seat like a child. "What happened?"

Lane told him.

"You should have killed him."

Catherine Dowd smiled, and nodded. "You certainly should have destroyed Reverend Parris, Mister Lane. It's what we pay you for, after all."

"Better than nothing, I suppose," Dowd said. "And, by God, I'd like to have seen it!"

Lane had heard that said before. He doubted that Dowd would really have enjoyed seeing it.

He picked up his reins, nodded to Mrs. Dowd, and said, "You'll keep those two men by you."

"Yes," Dowd said. "You can bet your bottom dollar on that!"

"A third man wouldn't hurt anything. Might help, as long as Pace runs lose. He won't waste time. And . . . today, I beat James Parris."

"We get your point." Mrs. Dowd said, and folded

167

her parasol. The sun was done. It was nearly dark. "And will you be able to kill Mister Pace, should you meet him, Mister Lane?"

"I don't know," Lane said. "I understand he's very quick."

"Yes," she said. "The difference between the quick and the dead." She looked down at her husband. "Matthew, I wonder if your cattle are worth all this fuss."

Dowd laughed, winking at Lane. "There's a woman for you, Regulator. Don't care for violence." He glanced up at his wife, the rounds of his pinch-nose glasses reflecting circles of dusk grey. "Every great venture, my dear, in business and otherwise, is founded in violence, though that may never be seen, never actually placed into action. Down here—it *may* be seen, be placed into action. That is no great difference."

"It seems a great difference to me," Catherine Dowd said. "To Mister Lane and that man from Texas, too, I expect. Matthew, I'm tired, and I wish to go home."

Dowd picked up the reins. "See if you can track that damn fellow down then, Lane. And, of course, be as careful as you can."

"Matthew."

"Very well, dear. Good night, Lane."

"Good night."

Lane sat the bay, watching the surrey out of sight down the ranch road, heading in. Dowd had been lucky that Pace had chosen—or Parris had chosen—the Short-C for his first killing. Lane didn't have much faith in those two drovers stopping Frank Pace from doing anything he wished to do. A third man riding guard might help: three against was long odds. Well, he'd have Shand see to it. Noddy Barkley was a tough kid, fair enough shot with a rifle. Shand might see to it the boy came off work for a few days, stayed close to the Dowds. Owen and Evans and the boy would make a fair three-man guard.

Not fair enough in the long run, of course, the long run being about another two days. In that time, were he in Pace's boots, he would have bumped another cattleman for sure, or one or two drovers—or little Matthew Dowd. Broken Iron was the biggest outfit in this county.

Pace would nail Dowd sure as shooting, three-man guard or not. Unless Lane killed him first or Harley Akins took a hand and made his play good.

Were he Dowd, he'd take his wife and get the hell out—go up to Boise, or up to Canada and stay for however long it took. It had always surprised Lane how slowly men saw the wisdom of running. Unless a fellow was a fighting man or thought he was, it was usually by far the smartest thing to do in a tight.

Shand and Lane, hired hands both, could run Iron well enough for a few months.

If Dowd weren't such a small man, he might be persuaded. As it was, the little man would have to take some chances for his big money.

Fair enough.

Lane cut off the road and booted the tired bay up into a canter, cutting across a field and through a patch of dwarf willow. It was a shorter way home.

169

Nothing past the willows but rolling grassland for a mile or just short of a mile. Then skirt Big Pond, then small pond. Up to the first corral fences, along them to the stables, the bunk-house, and bed.

"That hurt?" Shand said. Lane was sitting on a three-legged stool in his underwear pants. Shand sat on his bunk, behind him. He'd rubbed the cuts down Lane's side with brown soap and hot water. McCorkle had provided the hot water, but refused to doctor Lane's cuts. "When Cookie offers you a piece of his apple pie, take it," Shand had said, coming back to the bunk-house with the hot water. Now the cuts were clean, Shand was shaking up a brown bottle of screw-fly liniment.

"Use a lot of that," Lane said. He doubted the liniment would hurt as much as the scrubbing had.

He was wrong.

"You leave this doctoring to me," Shand said. "I've tended just about every kind of cut here is. A knife cut is nothing new to me." He shook the bottle again, pulled the cork with a "pop"—and poured what felt like fire down Lane's side.

"*Jesus!*"

A half hour later, Lane lay on his bunk in the moonlight, listening to Shand snore and feeling the slow easing of his muscles after the long day's riding. The cuts felt better—burned out and clean. he'd pour red-eye whiskey on them a time or two— would burn a good deal less than the liniment— and that would fix them up all right. "What are

170

you cussing about?" Shand had said. "You're damn sure safe from the screw-worm, anyway."

Lane had heard some drovers laughing at that on the other side of the partition and had called out, "I know that jackass laugh of yours, Turner, and I'll touch your fat butt up with a stock whip, you don't look out!"

The drovers had laughed harder at that, and ragged Turner until Shand went in to shut them up.

Now it was quiet. An ease-your-muscles cool and breezy mountain night. It was good sleeping up here, better than almost anywhere Lane had known. He might have slept better in the mountains of Mexico years ago, when he and Martin Brady were sitting guard on a gold mine. Proved to be not much gold in that mine, and no pay at all for guarding it. "After all," the *Patron* had said to them, "You were hired to guard gold. Now it appears that there was no gold! You have guarded nothing and must not expect to be paid for that."

There was a thief. And Brady, more Mex than American from having been raised there—a good gun—had still felt an obligation to the fellow.

Those were nights for sleeping, though. Twenty-three years old, tough as tough ever gets, with a belly full of mescal, beans, and chili peppers. Lying out in the *chaparral* with a skinny little Mexican girl, both of them wrapped in one of the big *Saltillo* blankets.

That was sleeping . . . on those cold, clear nights.

But this was all right. A long time later and a little way down. But all right.

He stretched carefully, favoring the cuts along his ribs. Then he turned on his other side, reached out to touch the butt of the Bisley Colt's on the stool beside his bunk, and went to sleep.

He dreamed no dream that he remembered.

When he woke, the moon was lower, no longer shining through the narrow bunk-house window. He lay for a minute, coming fully awake, listening to Shand's soft snoring. The cuts down his side felt better. The sharp, sudden little pains were gone.

Lane got out of bed, and collected his clothes and the Bisley Colt's without making any noise. Barefoot, he picked up his boots from beside his bunk, went to the partition door, opened it, and stepped quietly past the bunks of dark-blanketed cowpokers snoring and sighing in their sleep.

He soft-footed out the bunk-house door, down the steps, and into the yard, went to the pump bucket and found enough water to wash in without working the clanking pump handle. He washed there, in the moonlight, taking some care about it, dried himself with the worn pump towel, and dressed.

Lane looked up at the moon again, dug into his trouser pocket for his watch, and turned the face of it this way and that in the moonlight until he could read the time. Then he walked out of the yard and into the shadows beside the tack shed.

There were two men to take account of: Drew, up by the house; and Bobtail Jack, on the stable roof with a rifle. Three other drovers were riding circle a couple of hundred yards out. Jack was the one that concerned Lane. Old Bobby was a nice shot with a long gun and was liable to knock Lane over like a rabbit if he saw him clear in the moonlight down here.

Lane stuck to shadows. The drovers would have their eyes tuned to notice a man moving in toward, not away from, headquarters. So at least he hoped. Be some embarrassment to being shot in the butt by his own.

He had to cross two clear moonlit spaces to reach a patch of brush below the pines. Running would be too noisy; sneaking would take too long. Lane sauntered across the first—the lot back of the colt corral—as if he'd had an urge to stroll that far to pee. Once back in cover, he paused to wipe his face with his bandanna. His back had itched all the way over—a rifle-bead itch, it felt like.

In for a penny, in for a pound. Lane walked across the big holding pen even slower, his hands in his pockets. Not even that wall-eyed fool, Jack, would shoot a fellow strolling with his hands in his pockets . . .

Lane ducked through the pen fence and on into a tangle of thorn and Make-peace and was glad to be there, scratches and all. He crouched in the thicket for a few moments on one knee, considering how he'd skin Bobtail Jack in the morning for keeping such a shitty lookout. Fact was, what he'd managed foxing out Pace could manage foxing in. Have to put a man on the ground, that was all there was to it. Needed a man around these outbuildings just sitting quiet, with a shotgun across his lap.

Shand would grumble—all the guarding was costing him work not done, and the work would be piling up day by day. Dowd might put two cents in on that, as well; the little man hated to see any profit slide and there was no profit in drovers standing all night with rifles in their hands.

Still—needed another man out here. No doubt about it.

Lane got to his feet, and, taking some punishment from the briars, pushed his way through the scrub and out, under the first of the pinon pines that stood gathered on the rise back of the headquarters buildings.

Little of the moonlight filtered through the needle-furred branches, only some faint dappling, an occasional slight fall of silver light through a gap in the thick foliage thirty feet and more above the needle carpeted ground.

The air smelled of the mountains—a scent of high snow, and stone—and it smelled of pine.

A hunting owl moaned as it flew, a little way away.

Lane walked on, ducking his head to keep the pine boughs from his eyes where the trees grew close, climbing through the dappled light where the bigger trees stood far apart.

Then he saw her, standing, waiting for him.

She was laughing, standing in the little clearing bright with moonlight. "Oh," she said, as he walked up to her, "the funniest thing! Charlie Drew *caught* me! I'd just left the house by the kitchen door, and—" She hiccuped with laughter.

174

"Charley Drew was in the shadows by the corner there and he said . . ." She imitated Drew's Mississippi drawl. "Aw-right, yew son-of-a-bitch—reach!' "

"And *I* said: 'Charley, I'm just going out to pee.' God, Fen, you should have seen his face! I thought the poor man was going to dig a hole and hide!"

Lane reached out to hold her, hug her tight. "And what about Dowd?" he said, smelling the clean sweet smell of her hair.

Catherine leaned back in his arms, smiling up at him. "My dear," she said, "Don't you know that Matt knows all about this?"

"You tell him?"

"No." Her white face was shadowed by a pine branch just above them. "I've told you that he was asleep the times I've come out to you. Or he pretends to be—and I suppose I'm a bit of a coward; I let you think that."

Lane was amused. It had occured to him that Dowd must suspect something, but none of that had ever showed in the owner's manner toward him. It was possible that the little rancher was one of those men who enjoyed having their wives step out—enjoyed imagining, or being in the room, for that matter, seeing their wives with other men.

"Is he pleased?"

"No." Catherine nestled into his arms. "It hurts him terribly, I think. But he never talks about it. Never mentions it."

She'd brought an afghan wrapped around her shoulders like a shawl. Lane took it off her, and spread it on the ground.

"Come here," he said, and pulled her down beside her.

"This Texan," she said.

"Be still."

She sat, propped up on one arm, white face, white shoulders, the white silk of her negligee shining in the moonlight, while Lane untied the little bows that held the gown to her.

She was quiet, sitting still, watching his face as he undressed her.

He opened the gown and gently folded the soft material down her arms so that she sat before him naked to the waist, her breasts, soft and pale, soft nippled, sagging slightly with their weight. The silk of her gown lay puddled around her hips, the slight swell of her belly. Her navel was a shadowed dimple.

"You're one of the best I've ever seen," Lane said. "One of the most beautiful women."

"*One* of the best? That's not usually what's said, sir, to a lady one is about to mount!" She smiled at him. "Why should that compliment please me so, I wonder? Because you're being honest with me, I suppose, you strange man."

Lane began to stroke her shoulders, then bent to lift one of her heavy breasts to his mouth, and gently kissed the soft nipple. Then he bit lightly into the rich flesh.

She stroked his hair. "Is it true, you grizzled veteran, that you were once a *maquereau*—a fancy man? I suppose that was true . . ." She sighed as he stroked her breasts. "They're so big," she said, "I've sometimes been ashamed of them—the way

176

men look at me, as if I were some randy great cow, all udders and wet hindquarters." She kissed his hair. "Oh, be a little rough with me—I don't mind. These damn breasts the men love so much—they were meant for children, you know, not men at all. I feel a cheat with these bulging things, and never a child to suckle on them. I don't think Dowd can . . . or I, I don't know . . ."

Lane laid her down across the afghan's patterns and kissed her mouth. He kissed her for a while, stroking her rich breasts, the tender wisps of curls in her soft arm pits, kissing her throat, the neat small ears hidden as her hair fell loose and looser from its combs and pins. Her hair, when it was down, fell around her like a shawl, light brown, silken, shining in the moonlight.

Lane pulled away from her, stood and looked down at her for a moment, then took off his clothes. The night wind was cool, pouring through the pines like cool water, with the same sound that water might have made. It was darker now, the moon lower, shining more aslant through the trees.

When he stood naked, she came up onto her knees, the gown falling from her, and kneeling in front of him, began to kiss and lick at his cock, nuzzling its thick stiffness, sucking awkwardly at the tip.

Lane had taught her that the third time they were together. It was something she had learned to enjoy, as she had learned to enjoy other things he'd taught her.

A new-hired drover named Ledbetter had

absconded with six Broken Iron horses just a week or two after Dowd had brought Lane back from Boise. Lane had gone after the fellow who'd tried his damndest to be clever, and doubled back off Iron range to ride out east through Gunsight Gap. Lane had caught up with Ledbetter just the other side of the canyon, and Ledbetter had lost his wits and shown fight. Lane had waited till the drover emptied his revolver, then had ridden him down, knocking him off his horse. The fall had broken Ledbetter's collarbone, and Lane had thought best to let the rustling business go with that, and a beating. He'd beaten the drover with his belt, warned him out of the territory, and set him afoot, to walk his way to wherever.

It had taken all the rest of the day to gather the stampeded horses, and Lane had hobbled them and camped where he was near a creek called the Bright. In the morning, late, when he'd gathered the stock to go, he'd heard a woman singing. Catherine Dowd had come out of the Gap, picnicking, with her Indian girl. Mrs. Dowd had left the Iron early, and come on out to the Bright with a basket of sandwiches and fruit, and her water color paints.

Lane had gone down the creek to say howdy, and had stayed and visited with the women, and had an egg sandwich for his breakfast before he headed the horse herd back. He'd told Mrs. Dowd he'd lost the rustler—skedaddled—rather than tell her he'd beaten the man and that had been the story he'd stuck to with Dowd as well.

He'd met her the next time, riding up on the

west section, and they'd talked.

When a month later they'd met again—he riding out of town, she heading in in the trap—Lane had leaned from his saddle after they'd talked a while, and kissed her.

Shortly afterward, they'd become lovers.

He had taught Catherine what she was doing— she'd had, like many ladies, no real idea of love-making at all until they met—and she enjoyed it, was enjoying it now. She gripped him hard, her hands holding the backs of his thighs, and gently kissed at his cock, licking along it as he sighed with pleasure, his hand buried in her flowing hair.

After a while, as she sucked at him more strongly, more urgently, Lane gently pushed her away. She sat back on her naked haunches, looking up at him, her mouth wet, half open. "Christ," she said, "but I love that! I love it so."

"Lie down."

She lay down luxuriantly in the soft nest of her gown on the warm afghan, stretching her white arms up over her head, letting her long, sturdy legs fall wide apart so that he could see her secrets. The soft light brown curls that barely showed at her tender armpits were richer, thicker, between her legs. The hair grew up to a little point just below her navel, and only showed a soft parting, not the flesh of her cunt, lower down. For that, Lane had found to his pleasure, he had to search gently, parting the delicate fur, spreading it to find her meat.

He knelt between her legs and did that now,

stroking her thighs, stroking lightly down to her rounded calves, the fine-angled bones of her ankles. Then sliding his hands up again, cupping the curves of her legs, squeezing them gently, caressing her, petting her, bending to lick up along the smooth skin, up the straining tendon at her groin, then parted the thick hair there with his fingers until, even in the fading moonlight, he could see the wet lips, swollen and pouting apart.

He kissed her lightly there at first, licking at the damp fur, parting it with his fingers to get at her. Then he kissed her as he kissed her on the mouth, hard, forcing the lips wide open under his, driving his tongue deeper into her, forcing his face against her, opening her up wider until his tongue was buried in her, sucking the syrup out of her, drinking from her.

Catherine began to make her sound then, a sort of soft humming sound of pleasure as he worked at her. He enjoyed her that way for a while, sucking the sweetness of her as she began to twist and turn beneath him, as the long smooth strong thighs rose and clamped themselves to him and then fell away. He had to grip her hips hard, holding her down and still while he worked.

Now she was wet, her juices came flowing faster than he could lick them up—sticky, salt, and smelling slightly of blood.

"Oh, my dear—oh, my *dear!*" She twisted almost out of his hands, her fingers reaching down to tangle in his hair, pushing at his head, then tugging, holding him against her.

Her knees were up now, spread wide as she

could. He licked down into the soft crack of her buttocks, opening her with his hands.

Catherine cried out without words, and Lane, trembling, his cock up hard, swollen to bursting, moved up on his knees, found her with the tip and shoved it up into her with a rush.

Catherine Dowd threw her head back and screamed and brought both hands up to clamp across her mouth as Lane drove into her—and out almost entirely—and in again, driving up into her with all the length of it, with all his strength. Her soft breasts shook at each impact, trembling as he fucked her. Her long, full legs were swung up in the air, her feet arched, toes pointed in an agony of sensation.

Her wetness, the swollen cock thrusting into her, made a quick, rhythmic sucking sound, sticky and liquid, as loud as their gasping breaths.

Lane found himself moving on Catherine Dowd, shaking and desperately excited as a boy with his first woman. He fastened onto her, gripping her white breasts, biting and kissing her soft throat, doing all of that without thinking about it, without planning what he'd do next, and what after that, to give her joy.

Instead, it was all as natural, as thoughtless, as eating a fine breakfast would be to a starving man. He was used to giving great pleasure to women— it had, after all, been part of his business for many years—and used to getting pleasure from them as well.

But not like this.

This was so fine, felt so . . . *close*, that it scared

him. It frightened him and drove him on, deeper into her . . . and slower, slower, stretching out each moment as long as he could. The sweet smell of her, her smoothness, the squeezing heat and wet where her cunt gripped him—none of them meant as much to him as the look of her face in the moonlight. Her face, contorted with her pleasure, twisted in the agony of what he was doing to her—with her—and her eyes were wild with it.

Staring down into Catherine Dowd's face, Lane felt himself begin to go—begin to start sliding down a long, long slope. He tried for an instant to hold himself back, to hold still, to stop thrusting into her, and he couldn't.

She reached up and wrapped her arms around him. "Oh, dear God, I love you . . ."

Lane felt himself going . . . everything slipping away as he went. A river of silver came flowing up out of him, and he cried out like a child, as the river ran.

He stayed with her, lying on her, for some little time, feeling the slow ebb of jissom from him, the slow heartbeat contractions of her cunt around him. Catherine hugged him close, and said nothing to him.

Then, slowly . . . slowly, Lane pulled out of her, and felt the warmth and wet, the delicate lips of her sex squeezing closed as he left her. He rolled off of her, and lay stretched out at her side.

For a while, a few minutes, they lay still, listening to the night wind rising now toward dawn, sighing through the pines above them. It was chilly, and Lane turned to her, propped up on his elbow, and tugged a fold of the afghan over her. She reached up and touched the long scar that ran down his left cheekbone.

"Your poor body," she said, and lightly stroked along his chest touching the thin, ridged knife scar that traced across it. "I hate the men who hurt you so. Damn them! Are they dead?"

"Most."

"Good." She lay watching him in the dimming, shadowed light. "I suppose that your name is not really Fenton Lane?"

"I love you, Catherine," Lane said, looking down at her—and was as surprised and embarrassed as if he'd farted. He'd thought, by God, that he was long past that particular jackassery.

But she said nothing to him in reply, as if she hadn't heard him, and went on with what she'd been saying. "Is it your name?"

"No."

"Matthew thinks that you're a man named Hondo Lane. A gunman from Arizona. That's what he tells everybody."

Lane laughed. "Honey, Hondo Lane was as big as a house, twice my size. And he turned rancher long ago. I met the fellow once, in Nebraska Territory . . ."

"A nice man?"

"I'd say so. Good to dogs, anyway; always had a bunch around him."

"But was not you."

"Not me."

"Well, I won't tell Matthew. He depends on things like that to keep his feelings . . . steady."

She sat up, tugging the afghan up around her naked shoulders. "You haven't asked—and I've appreciated that . . . about Matthew and me." She turned to look into Lane's face, her own thrown into shadow by the setting moon. "Matthew . . . was always a friend. Our families knew each other . . . and I was kind to him, when we were young. I didn't tease him as the other children did. I suppose the boys his age were very cruel to him; he was tiny, even then, a sad little doll of a boy all dressed up in a Fauntleroy suit, poor thing . . ."

She sighed. "Well, in due time, years later, a terrible thing happened to our family . . . a terrible thing." She looked down, and her long hair, loose, fell over the side of her face like a curtain. "My father—a most wonderful man, a shipowner out of Victoria, always brought us the most marvelous presents, things his captains had brought back from the Indies . . . from China. Well, one morning, in midsummer, my father woke up—and he was mad. We were downstairs, having breakfast, and we heard the oddest kind of singing. It didn't sound like Father at all. And a few minutes later he came down the stairs, and he was carrying mother in his arms . . . and he'd cut her throat with his razor. And he said, with precisely the same funny face he used when he was telling us a funny story about . . . oh, Chinese merchants, or some of his sailors who had had too much to drink, and had done something ridiculous—with just that sort of face, he looked at us, holding Mother in his arms, and said: 'Children, your mother doesn't want any breakfast—not even toast and jam.' "

184

She glanced up at Lane. "It . . . that thing happening, ruined us all. My family had been a large family . . . cousins . . . uncles, aunts. People pointed to us in the streets . . . whispered about us.

"Matthew did not. He knew all about being pointed to in the street, being whispered about. As the years went by, we came to depend upon him. He would bring his brake 'round and take us for rides in the country . . . picnics. My sisters and I grew very fond of Matthew. He was like a . . . a lifeline, I suppose. He visited almost every day . . . joking . . . bringing little presents for Susannah, for all of us. We became his family, I believe.

"My father had been locked in a madhouse for four years, when Matthew Dowd asked me to marry him. I could not say 'no' to him."

She started to stand up, and Lane held out his hand to help her. "It's getting late," she said. "Time for me to embarrass poor Charley again with some out-house humor."

As they got dressed, Lane watched, in the failing light, as she drew her gown over that long, full, white nakedness, picked up the afghan and draped it over her shoulders. Then he got his boots on, stomping each foot in turn for a fit.

He took her hand, and they started walking down out of the grove, going carefully in the near dark. The moon was down, dawn something more than an hour away.

"Listen, my knight with no name," she said, "I have been thinking of two things—and now I want you to think of them." She tripped a little over a fallen branch, and Lane gripped her hand harder, and lifted it to support her. "First, I have begun to think that Matthew Dowd and I can remain friends, and care for each other, without playing at husband and wife. Money has begun to mean a great deal to Matthew; I doubt it would break his heart if we were to part. And the other thing that I've been thinking . . . is that Norah Chamblee is dying, the poor, poor dear. She is dying, and Clive will be taking her back to her people in Pennsylvania soon. She wants to be with them."

Lane saw her pale face turn toward him in the darkness.

"Clive Chamblee is looking for a couple to take on his horse ranch, to manage it for him and to become his partners. I don't think poor Clive will ever want to come west again, not without Norah."

They were out of the grove, at the edge of the pines by the feed lot. It was very dark. Catherine reached up to put her arms around Lane's neck, and kissed him. Then she said, "Now, you think about those two things, sir," and turned to go, but stopped after a few steps. Lane could see the white of her gown. Her voice came softly out of the dark.

"Can you kill that Texan?"

"I believe I can."

"Well, see that you do it," she said.

EIGHT

PACE GOT out to Mrs. Phelps' well before dawn.

It had been a long ride from Breckinridge's—from the Short-C, since Breckinridge no longer owned it, or anything. Pace had learned early that some few hours of cooling out after a piece of work was the best way to avoid unpaid-for trouble. Those hours gave hot-heads a space to cool down, gave the law a chance to think twice, too.

Once, in Texas, Pace had killed two men, store keepers, and then had ridden straight into Waco, had supper, and gone to bed. He'd been half asleep when he heard a bunch come howling up the hotel stairway, shotguns, rifles, and ropes ready.

Pace had fired through the cheap deal door to make them think and had piled out the window, across an echoing tin roof, and made it to the stable and his horse in his long underwear. He'd had his revolver, his purse, and his hat and had ridden hard out of town in that fashion.

None of the men in that crowd would have dared to face him, alone. No three of them would have dared.

It had been a lesson to him and worth more than

had been left behind at the Acme Hotel. From then on, Pace had done his work and let a few hours pass before he showed his face. It kept things more a matter of business. Less a matter of pride and temper.

So he had ridden wide around Grover, coming in from the Short-C, and had holed up in an aspen grove to rest the dun and have a nap of his own. He'd watered the horse at a little branch, stepped upstream a few feet and lain down to take a long, long drink himself. He felt fine.

He'd ridden just a short way further up the branch, and found a ruin where some settler had built a cabin in a wild green aspen grove. A likely spot. Pace had hobbled the dun, and then stretched out on the rough grass in the shade, his hat down over his eyes, and slept deep through the evening and on into the night.

The coolness woke him at moonrise, and he got up and walked to a patch of brush, dropped his trousers, and crapped. He wiped himself with a bunch of leaves—a boy he'd known, growing up, had used a bunch of poison oak leaves for that purpose, and had become famous locally for having done that—pulled up his trousers and gone to unhobble the dun.

Time and time enough to ride back to town and stop off at Mrs. Phelps'. Had been some twelve hours now since Breckinridge was shot—and those drovers done. Anyone looking for trouble now would be looking for it despite any passage of time.

Pace was concerned to see the Porter girl. He

felt, he *knew*, she must be misjudging him for his roughness with her. If she would listen to him, then she'd understand how an intelligent fellow, insulted and surprised, might act the rough.

There was something about the girl; she seemed to cut an odd line between living as a whore and as a lady. Pace thought that a woman like that, fine as she might be but still a split-tail, could understand a man who, while yearning for higher things, while enjoying the riches of literature and so forth, might still find a necessity in killing.

"I'm a complicated man," he said to himself, guiding the dun through dappled moonlight. "I may find understanding in the heart of a complicated woman." He thought she had liked him well enough out in the country when he had killed the two drovers for her. Possibly that had been why she'd been so rude and accusing at Mrs. Phelps'. Had liked a fellow, found some noble quality in him, and had been confused to see him come into a whorehouse with a stiff in his trousers.

For a girl forced into that trade, a girl who might have seen the hope of rescue by a decent man, not afraid of a fight, such disappointment could have been cause enough for rudeness and taunting.

She'd misjudged him, and that was that. And, thinking her nothing but a down whore, he had misjudged her as well. Many great loves and kindnesses had begun in that fashion, with mistakes. You read it all the time.

But he shouldn't have cut her and there was no way of saying he should. She had an apology due for that and he would make it handsomely.

Pace took advantage of the moonlight, rode north to cut the Grover road, found it, and set the dun to a canter, heading in.

Near two hours later a moon-down, he tied the dun to a picket fence and walked up to Mrs. Phelps' back door.

He knocked, and an Indian woman came to open to him.

Pace had thought of asking for the girl right off —then he thought better of that. "Get Mrs. Phelps."

There was a lamp on a side table just inside the door. By that light, Pace saw the Indian woman walk away down a short hall and, a minute or two later, saw Mrs. Phelps coming. She looked upset.

"Oh, Jesus," she said. "Will you please, *please*, get the hell away from here?"

"I want to—"

"The marshal is in here! And his deputy is, too. Now Mister Pace, will you please *leave.*" The old woman looked like a clown, pasty pale under her rouge.

"I want to see Miss Porter," Pace said. "There won't be any trouble. I'm just going to apologize to her for my behavior."

Mrs. Phelps looked even worse as she stood there.

"Mister Pace," she said. "I will pay you a hundred dollars if you will go away. I promise I'll have that sum right over to your hotel in gold or greenbacks as you please if you will go away." She appeared to have a second thought, once she'd said it. "And if you'll promise not to come back to his house, ever."

She was making Pace angry.

"Listen," he said, and he leaned into the doorway, the crown of his hat brushing the top of the door frame, "you ask Miss Porter to come here to talk with me and there won't be any trouble."

"The marshal—"

"Do it right away," Pace said, and there was an expression on his face that kept Mrs. Phelps from saying anything more.

She nodded, and turned and went off down the hall. Pace noticed the old woman had a little hump on her back, high up, between her shoulder blades —that, or she was walking hunched over, worried.

He stood there in the doorway for a couple of minutes, waiting for Marcia Porter.

Then, when he was about to go inside to get her, she stepped into the hall and walked toward him. She had a robe or wrapper on, with Chinese dragons sewn on it in gold thread. She looked very pretty, as pretty as he had remembered. Her dark hair shone in the lamplight. She didn't look angry.

She looked a little afraid, and Pace smiled at her, to show he meant no harm. She was little as a minute—stood no higher than his chest as she came up to him. Cutting a girl like this had been a poor thing to do, he thought, something that a man who *was* a man would admit to. He could see the small scab, high on her left cheek. You could barely see it.

"I'd like to tell you," Pace said, as she stood looking up at him, "that I deeply regret what I did

—forcing you that way. It was not . . . that was not the act of a gentleman."

He waited, then, to see what she would say, but she didn't say anything. She still seemed mighty shy, or nervous about something. He saw tiny beads of sweat across her forehead.

"I said you don't have to be scared of me," Pace said. "What's done is done, and I own my fault. Now we can just sit down and talk, if you want, and I don't expect the other at all. Our friendship is more valuable to me than that sort of thing. I'm a reading man, you see, and a fine friendship is as good as anything there is between two people . . . that have had hard times; I reckon I understand hard times as good as anybody."

He smiled at her again, but she didn't smile back.

"Mister . . ." Behind him. "If you do anything quick, I'm goin' to cut you in two pieces."

Usually when someone said something of the sort to Pace, he turned and killed them. He had been hurt only once doing that, and he hadn't been hurt badly.

This time, though, he stayed where he was for a moment, looking down at the girl. She was panting with fear; he could see a delicate vein jumping in her throat.

"Forced you into it?" he said.

She just stared up at him.

"Don't you be frightened," Pace said to her. "I don't blame you. I care for you. You've found a true friend in me."

The girl threw back her head like a drinking

bird, and screamed, "Kill him, Harley! Oh *kill him!*" And she backed down the hall, staring at Pace.

Pace smiled at her, to let her know he understood; waited until she had reached the hall door and gotten through it, then slowly turned around.

It was the deputy who had threatened him—the Yankee bar-fighter with the belly. He stood down the steps and to one side, off the walk. He was holding a double barreled shotgun, a twelve-gauge. Pace couldn't tell what make it was.

Now Pace was facing the man, and he would have drawn and killed him, but he saw Harley Akins standing on the other side of the yard. Akins was wearing a black suit. He didn't have a hat on. His white shirt front and a small brass star on his suit lapel both picked up reflected moonlight.

Pace looked at Akins carefully—saw that he was young, and calm—looked a hard-case, as told. Wore a shoulder holster. And was standing near forty feet away. Shy . . . or a sure-shot who enjoyed the edge that distance gave him. Not shy, Pace felt.

"Pace," Akins said, "Shed that revolver belt."

"Make me," Pace said. This looked to be a lark. Kill the fat deputy moving, then try Mister Marshal Sure-shot. That boy need a lesson about forcing girls into betrayal.

"There'll be no shooting here, Pace," Akins said, his voice carrying over the sound of a light breeze drifting through trees in the darkness behind him. "Unless you force it."

"That so?" Pace said, and would have drawn and killed the deputy, but he saw Akins start to take his suit coat off. That was odd, and Pace held up, watching.

Harley Akins took his suit coat off, folded it, and laid it in the grass. Then he unbuckled his shoulder holster—the weapon seemed to Pace to be some sort of foreign pistol; the angle of the grip was strange—and put that down on the folded coat.

"Pace," Akins said, "drop that revolver belt or Meagher will kill you."

"Say what?" Pace said, smiling.

"Either Meagher will kill you or I will beat you. Take your choice."

A fight then. It was very odd, but Pace felt pleased enough. He enjoyed a fight, had killed some men with his hands in the past. A fight might be enjoyable. And, if he was careful and didn't kill Akins, the whole matter might be better than a shooting. No use having to ride around this territory in future . . .

"And what about Fatty?" he said.

"Kiss my butt-hole," the deputy said, and tightened his grip on the shotgun. He was peering hard through the moonlight to see a move that Pace might make.

"Meagher," Akins said to him, "if he drops that gunbelt, you take the shotgun off him. And win or lose, don't throw down on him again."

"Shit," the deputy said.

"Do what I tell you, or take off that badge."

"Makin' a mistake, Har'."

"Do it."

The deputy stepped one step back, and the

muzzle of the shotgun slowly dipped an inch or two.

"My, oh my," Pace said. He hoped that Marcia Porter would be watching. Akins was young for his job, after all. Other places, other people involved, Pace would have already shot the boy and his fat deputy, just as soon as that foreign pistol had been laid on the ground; just as soon as the shotgun muzzle had lowered. Pace suspected that Akins would have done the same, wouldn't have risked a rough-house, if the girl hadn't been the subject of it.

Akins proved him right.

"I'm going to teach you not to go cutting women with a knife," he said.

Pace heard a window opening in the house above him. The ladies would be looking. "Now, I don't think Marcia minded all that much," he said to Akins, and unbuckled his gunbelt, and let the revolver and big Bowie slide to the door sill. Then he walked down the steps and out into the yard, paying no more attention to the deputy. He took off his hat, and tossed it aside. "We are going to have a union of the heart, you see. Something you wouldn't understand."

Akins came for him at a run.

Pace had half a foot of height on the marshal, and likely some pounds as well. There was more than enough moonlight to see by.

Akins came running, but not wild. Pace figured the boy was a city brawler, probably had handled those chores for Segrue at Fort Smith. Stocky. Looked strong, too. It all looked to be a lark.

Akins hit him head down, and very hard, and drove Pace back across the yard, his breath knocked out of him. Pace had been kicked by horses harder, but could not recall such a blow from a man. It had cracked a rib for him; he had felt it give.

Going to be a considerable lark.

Pace back-stepped as fast as he could to get some room to set himself, but Akins was right after him, striking at his face with short, sharp punches. They were the kind of punches that a prize fighter used—thoughtful blows that had been considered, however quickly, and then delivered. Pace threw his arms up to protect his face. His face had grown numb; he heard a humming sound.

When he put us his arms, Akins struck him in the belly—the same swift, short punches.

The boy was hurting him, no saying he was not.

Pace reached down, caught Akins' left fist in his hand, bent his head quickly and, as the marshal struck at him, clubbed at him with his other fist, Pace bit Akins' hand to the bone. He ground his teeth into the hand, and felt blood flood into his mouth, twisted his head to drive his teeth in deeper, chewing, chewing. A small bone broke between his teeth. He bit deeper.

Harley Akins stopped striking him, trying to wrench his hand away—Pace felt him stop that, felt the boy set himself—and Akins kicked him in the stones.

For an instant, Pace felt nothing but the impact. Then he felt the pain. His body bent down in a bow despite him, his jaws still clamped on the marshal's hand.

A considerable lark.

Pace found that he couldn't move his legs for this while, but his hands were free. Akins kicked him again, twice, at the joint of his left knee. Pace felt the blows, reached up to his mouth, gripped Akins' hand, all slippery with blood, found its fingers, and broke one. He gripped another finger to break it but the blood made it slippery and difficult to grasp. Akins hit Pace across the back of the neck with his fist, and Pace fell to his knees. He felt something in Akins' hand part under his teeth—a blood vessel, or something else—and his teeth ground down and through another little bone.

Akins beat him and beat him as he knelt there, wrenching to tear the hand free, but Pace had it and held it in his jaws and chewed deeper and deeper into it.

Akins leaned in close to try for Pace's eyes with his free hand, trying to get a thumb into one of Pace's eyes but when Pace reached up for that hand, Akins jerked it away.

The marshal struck at Pace, and kicked him as he knelt in the yard and tried desperately to tear his hand free, out of Pace's jaws.

Akins was sobbing for breath. He was no longer moving so swiftly, striking such measured blows. He was anchored now to Pace, to the wreckage of his hand.

Pace heard someone, a woman, shouting from the house.

He felt pretty well. The pain in his groin was less. He felt all right. He glanced up and saw Akins' face as he swung his fist down at him. Pace didn't mind the blow; he cared more for what he saw in Akins' face.

The marshal was afraid.

Pace set himself, let the marshal's hand fall from his mouth, and slowly got to his feet. He was smiling.

"Harley . . . *Harley!*" It was the deputy with the shotgun.

Pace looked into Akins' face and saw the marshal hesitate, then glance over at his man and shake his head. Then he looked back at Pace and their eyes met for an instant. Pace nodded to him, stepped in, and hit Akins in the face. Akins forgot himself and struck at Pace with his left hand; it hit Pace's face in a splatter of blood and broken bones, and Pace heard the marshal cry out in agony.

Pace hit the marshal in the face again and knocked him staggering back. Akins put up his ruined hand to guard, and struck out with his right. He was trying to hit Pace in the Adam's apple to choke him.

Pace dodged that by a little, and hit Akins in the face once more. Akins kicked at him and swung his right fist at Pace's throat again, but the marshal's balance, his leverage for hard hitting, was all spoiled. His left hand hung ruined at his side, spattering black blood in the moonlight.

Still, he came at Pace, striking with his right fist, clawing once to try to get a thumb into Pace's eye and kicking hard at Pace's privates and the joints of his knees. Pace stepped aside from all that, measured the marshal as Akins came after him again, and struck him in the face with his left and then his right fist.

Akins staggered, but did not fall down, and Pace followed him and hit him again; he felt Akins' teeth break under the blow.

Akins lowered his head and drove into Pace to knock him down so he could put his boots to him, but Pace brought his knee up into the marshal's face, and Akins fell to one knee in the yard, put his left hand down to save himself from falling, and cried out as it touched the grass.

The woman called again from the house above them.

Pace kicked Akins in the side, in the small ribs. He stepped back for room, then back in and kicked Akins again. Akins gasped, and heaved himself back up on his feet. As he turned to face Pace coming in, Pace ducked the marshal's right-hand blow, grappled with him, reached down between them as they struggled, fumbled at Akins' groin, found the bulge of his privates, gripped it, clenched his fist with all his strength, and crushed Akins' nuts.

Harley Akins stiffened in Pace's grip, and screamed like a woman. Pace let loose, and Akins fell away from him, thrashing, twisting in the dirt of the yard.

Above them, a woman screamed as Akins had screamed.

Pace turned and looked at the big-bellied

deputy. The deputy stared at him for a moment, then put the shotgun down on the walk, and ran to Akins. Pace saw moonlight reflecting on tears in the fat man's eyes as he hurried by.

Pace walked back toward the whore house steps, holding himself hard, so as not to limp. The marshal had put some hurting on him, no lie. Pace stopped where he saw his hat lying in the dirt in the moonlight—moon was near set, near full dark —and carefully bent down to pick it up. Straightening up hurt worse than the bending had.

Pace heard the deputy trying to comfort Akins behind him. Then the back door of the house flew open and Marcia Porter came running out into the night. The dragon-sewn robe shone a moment in the lamplight from the open door behind her.

She ran across the yard to Akins and knelt beside him in the dark weeping. Pace was mighty impressed with her. Not every girl—roughened by the life, at that—would have hurried to comfort an injured man who had wronged her, forced her into a trick of betrayal.

It showed a tender heart, and that pleased him. And after all, the fellow might have meant something to her in the past. Pace thought of walking over there to say something to her, then decided not. A woman's ways were a woman's ways—best to go light over rough ground.

He went up onto the porch, found his gunbelt, and buckled it on. The cracked rib gave him some trouble with that, but nothing severe. That done, he went on down the walk in the darkness, paying no heed to the fussing around Akins over there. He found the dun, untied him, and climbed aboard. Knee hurt him, doing that.

He rode the dun on down a narrow track, leaving the lights and women's voices, the deeper voice of the fat deputy, behind him. Then he turned the horse's head to town.

Not such a lark, after all. Akins had been rough as a tree with the bark on. Too bad, though, he hadn't been careless with his gunhand. Had he been, Akins' shooting days would be gone and past. As it was, Pace doubted the marshal would ever strike some rowdy drunk left-handed. His boxing days were done. More than likely, with a pack of noisy whores seeing it—Marcia Porter excepted—the news of his beating would be all over the county by the end of the day coming, and be news enough to cost him his badge sooner or later. Folks didn't care for rough marshals who had proved not rough enough.

Pace was damn glad to see the lights on the porch of the Grover House. There'd been people out on the streets, some men with lunch pails going to work. A few had turned to watch him as he'd ridden by, so there'd been talk about Breckinridge's death—and the others. No talk yet about the fight with Akins.

But that would come. And when it did, and the news of two or three more cattlemen killed—then, it would be getting on time to take his money and ride back out through Gunsight Gap.

The job would be done by then, though. The sheep people might not rule the range in this country, but they'd have their right to graze, that was for sure.

Riding the dun in had been no pleasure. Pace ached from knees to topknot, and the rib was giving him trouble; it needed binding. He guided the dun up to the hotel porch, pulled the Spencer out of its bucket, and swung down. The hotel's boy ran down the steps to take the dun's reins and lead him out back to the stable. Pace reached out to stop the boy as he started off, dug in his vest pocket, and handed the kid, a sad little cross-eyed specimen, a two-bit piece. The boy made a little bow and thanked him.

Then, shouldering the rifle, Pace went up the steps and into the lobby. The natty young desk clerk was on night duty, and Pace went up and leaned on the desk.

"I want a hot water bath, up in my room."

"Well, Mister Pace, we generally find it more convenient for our guests to use the laundry shack—"

"Up in my room. A big wash tub, and a lot of hot water for it." He started to turn away, then glanced back. "That nigger, Bobby, around?"

"Yes, sir," the clerk said, and kept his eyes lowered. He rang the desk bell.

Pace climbed the stairs up to his room, feeling each step in his knees. That badge-boy had damn near kicked Pace's knees right off him.

In his room, Pace propped the Spencer in a corner, loosed his gunbelt and hung it over a chair back beside the bed, and lay down with a grunt of relief.

He was not used to feeling so worn from a fist fight.

He lay there for a while, watching the night black slowly lighten outside his window. He thought about Marcia Porter for awhile. It was said, though he'd never cared to believe it, that whores—used-to-be-whores—made a man the finest wife he could find. Had all the wild already out of her . . . was grateful for the chance to be a decent woman, and so forth.

He supposed it might be true. One thing was sure; Marcia was a reading girl. She was a girl who read good books, or would like to if she had the chance. Pace had noticed that people's good sense showed in their eyes. Fools, now, had the eyes of fools.

The girl had good brains in her head; it showed in her eyes.

Akins had had some brains in his, too. The look that had passed between them when that fat deputy had called out . . . and Akins knowing damn well he was licked.

Give the kid credit—he didn't squeak for the shotgun.

Pace imagined the marshal fucking Marcia Porter. He supposed they had done it, at least once or twice. That old fireship Phelps would have forced the girl to it. Doubted the girl enjoyed it much.

A knock on the door. Pace sat up and pulled the Remington from its holster on the chair.

"Come on in."

It damn sure wasn't black Bobby that came through the door with the first steaming pail of hot.

It was the Reverend Parris, up early and looking like something the cat dragged in. Not that Pace felt he was any fashion plate, either; chops felt about double normal size.

"What the hell do you want?" he said to Parris. He was anxious for that hot bath.

"Now, what do you imagine, Mister Pace?" the Reverend said, standing in the doorway like an actor. He looked poorly, for sure. Busted nose, and a cheek cracked in—face blue and fat as a big city copper. His voice was strange, too. Had a honk in it, like a goose.

"I was beaten and maimed yesterday afternoon by that vicious hoodlum that Dowd employs."

There was a change, and Pace was amused by it.

"What?" he said. "Not by that grizzly old rounder you told me about, the scarred-up drifter Dowd bought up cheap?"

Parris came in and shut the door behind him, and Pace began to despair on his bath.

"The man attacked me while I was unarmed," Parris said, and began to pace up and down the room. "He had just attacked the high camp, burned it, and shot one of my men. Crippled the poor fellow for life, I believe. Unfortunately, I arrived just to late to prevent the attack." He gestured oddly with a narrow fist, and bobbed his damaged head. "Just too late!"

"Hold on, now," Pace said, interested. "This man hit a sheep camp?"

"The devil!" Parris said, honking like a goose. No question that busted nose was cramping his pulpit style. "I rode him down, though, faced him and took my whip to him!"

It occurred to Pace not by any means for the first time that this was a singular employer. He lay in his bed, the Remington still negligently in his hand, and heard this oddity out.

"You went after him and hit him with a whip? And you were unarmed?"

"I'm not poltroon, Mister Pace," said the goose. "I will punish any man where punishment is due."

"I see," Pace said, and got up off the bed. He'd had enough of Parris—and had something to think about beside. Whoever the man was working for the cattleman, Dowd, he was at least a little more than a beat-down drifter. Pace would have given something to have a talk with the herder the fellow'd shot. Could have told a lot from hearing that.

"Well," he said, "I've had a little ramble of my own—"

Parris stopped his pacing. "Yes," he said. "Breckinridge." He looked as pleased as his face would let him. "That was damn well done, sir!" And he advanced upon Pace like an actor on the stage to shake his hand. Pace let him shake away.

"Just had a fight with Marshal Akins," he said.

Parris looked much less pleased. "Not killed him!" he said.

"No. Ruffled him a bit."

"Well, thank God for that. The Marshal is . . . may be partial to our faction."

Pace supposed Parris meant because of Marcia Porter's flock of sheep. Doubtful any town marshal would choose up sides for any such reason as that.

"Not killed?"

"No."

Knock on the door.

"Come on in," Pace called. "Everybody else has."

And there was old Bobby, hefting the first smoking bucket. The cross-eyed little horse-holder was right behind him two-handing another, probably hoping for another two-bits for it.

"Now, I'm about to have a bath, Mister Parris," Pace said. "We can have a talk at dinner, if you like. I'll be downstairs about then." Should more than hint the man on his way.

"We have things to discuss, Pace," Parris said, with a look at Bobby and the boy as Pace motioned them in.

"About two o'clock in the afternoon, Mister Parris," Pace said, and limped over to stand by the door. "Down in the dining room, if you like or whereever."

Parris came to the door at last, and paused to turn his head and whisper like a convict to Pace as he went past. "*Matters to discuss . . .*"

"Yes, indeedy," Pace said, and closed the door after him. "Bobby," he said, "I'm going to need a half dozen of those buckets, hot as blazes. And the damndest wash tub you can find."

A half hour later, grey morning light at the room

window, the sounds of bustle wagons, riders, and boot heels—from outside it, Pace felt as near to heaven as he ever expected to get.

He lay only slightly bent, knees up, in a wash tub big enough for four Irishwomen working at once. The water was hot to steaming, and seemed to draw all the hurt out of his bones and muscles. He was soaping himself with lazy motions of a big yellow cake of lye soap, and stretching in the tub now and then, splashing some water on the floor, to crack his joints. Heavens, likely, had nothing to match it.

The old black man, Bobby, sat on a chair in a corner, waiting to bind up Pace's chest.

Bobby felt that Pace had not cheated him—had always paid his freight for any errand. Been generous, in fact. Still, Pace appeared to Bobby one of the worst white men he'd ever seen. And he'd seen a bunch. Not that Pace had struck him, or been rude and called him names, and certainly not that Pace had shot another white man, Breckinridge.

Pace had spoiled eyes. Ju-ju eyes.

Bobby thought he might be *Samedi* in another skin. He would be happy to bind up that white chest and leave this room. Pace was worst white man Bobby had seen since Able Wilkes had fallen off his horse at Fair Oaks and broken his neck.

NINE

THIS TIME, Lane took the pie.

McCorkle had hesitated, offering it, apparently of two minds whether Lane was worth it. What decided him, Lane thought, was the justice Lane had done to breakfast, tucking in four fried eggs, a pound of bacon, three biscuits, and a pile of hashbrown potatoes.

McCorkle had waited to see whether he would finish it up, and Lane did, beating out Henry Budd, a halfbreed horsebreaker from Tascosa, by a single biscuit.

Then, with Henry up and gone out into the grey dawn to gentle a horse named Peppermint, and Lane the last man sitting in the shed, McCorkle had sighed, turned from his stove to his pie safe, and hauled out a giant apple pie.

Still sighing, regretful, he sliced a wedge— bigger than necessary—out of it, cut a chunk of hoop-cheese to top, and laid this, in a tin plate, in front of Lane. Then he stood back to watch.

Lane made no sign that any test was intended, and ate the pie. Forked, chewed, and swallowed it down. Fine tasting—hard swallowing.

He finished it, grunted, "Fine pie," and managed

to get up from the long bleached wood table and lumber outside. He made it to the empty bunkhouse, fell into his cot, and slept another two hours.

The pleasures of being a Regulator.

When he woke, Lane lay in his bunk for a while, thinking. *"Can you kill that Texan . . . ? Well, see that you do it."* An interesting woman; more than interesting. And the mention of the Chamblee place . . . a horse ranch for the two of them to run and maybe own someday.

An interesting woman. And the first female he'd said "I love you" to in quite a number of years. Made a damn fool of himself, no doubt. And perhaps make a damneder fool of himself by being ashamed of it.

Hard to say why he'd said it. Heat of the moment, to be sure—and he liked her. Always had liked her, from the first time he'd seen her sketching by that river. No spring chicken of course . . . a woman full grown and then some. Looked mighty pretty sitting on the grass by that stream drawing away, all attention, all concentration. Flowers on her dress, some sort of little red flowers in a pattern all over the muslin . . . Been a breeze blowing then, stirring the cloth. Indian woman unpacking the lunch.

Pleasant day. And he'd liked her from the start. Thought she'd liked him, too. None of that niceynicey stuff so many decent woman canted at a man who wore a revolver. Straightforward as a man.

Beautiful. Fact was, he could have made a small fortune with her in San Francisco, times gone by.

Denver, too. "A pearl," something of a fine whore's way of talking—direct and knowing, smart. No fool. "Well, see that you do." Kill the Texan.

Lane got up off the bunk, stretched, buckled his gunbelt on, and strolled out to the pump for a drink. The big breakfast was sitting easier now.

The bright sunlight made him squint when he went out the bunk-house door, down the steps into the yard. Lane could see the Old Man looming miles away, clear as fine crystal in the high mountain air. Supposed that snow had lain on those peaks since time began—all those years, cooling the winds blowing down onto Grover, and the wilderness before there was any Grover, and Broken Iron. Before white men, maybe before Indians, too.

He worked the clanking pump a time or two, and gushed up a little run of ice-cold water. It tasted of stone—the best water he'd drunk since Sweet Springs, out of Denver nearly twenty years before. Holliday'd been there for the cure. Next to last cure, as it turned out.

Holliday'd hated it. Not much in the way of action in Sweet Springs. Lane supposed that Holliday might be living yet, if he could have stood quiet and rest.

Lane shook out his bandanna, wiped water from his mouth, and stood considering, listening to the sound of a buck saw. Couple of hands in the pit, working out planking.

Kill the Texan. Better to quit dreaming of the Lady Fair and think a bit on how to slay that damn

210

dragon. No question Pace would lie up for today, be seen around town, face anyone down who might care to question him. Unless Akins cared to question him. Damn if Lane could see how the marshal was going to stay clear of this business. Even if that Porter girl's being a sheeper would tend to keep him clear, it was hard to see how Grover could hold two such stud ducks without trouble coming.

Be nice to think that such trouble would save other trouble. But Akins just wasn't man enough to take on Frank Pace—unless he caught him on the sly, or at a goodly distance. With Segrue to tell him how, and back him—then, Akins might have been able to settle Frank Pace's hash.

But not alone and for sure not with that potbelly Meagher. A good enough policeman to patrol the shops; not good enough for serious fighting.

No, Akins wouldn't be doing Lane's job for him even if he gave it a try.

Lane walked to the out-house, closed the door behind him, hung his gunbelt on a nail, tugged his trousers down, sat on a cut-out, and enjoyed a very pleasant crap. Had known a man shot to death through a crapper door. Poor sapling never had a chance at all.

Lane doubted that Pace had that sort of sense of humor.

Pace would lie low today—probably had stayed out of town yesterday, after he'd killed Breckinridge. Smart men let towns cool down after a killing.

He'd lie low today, and tomorrow he'd come out

to Broken Iron. Tomorrow, or tomorrow night. He'd be coming for Dowd. And if Parris had anything to say about it, he'd be coming for Lane, too. Not likely Parris would forgive that beating. Not likely at all.

Lane tore some pages off the Sears & Roebuck catalogue, wiped himself, pulled up his trousers and buckled on his gunbelt. He left the out-house, and headed for the corrals.

He just didn't see sitting out here waiting for Pace to make his move. May as well be honest; he couldn't afford to let Pace make the try, couldn't let Pace choose the time and the way. If he did, Pace would likely kill him.

Lane hoped that Diller had reshod the pinto. Hooves needed trimming, too. Diller was a good farrier, but something of a bully. Liked to use his smith's muscles on men who didn't have them.

No, couldn't wait even another day. It was go in after the Texan or run.

And it would be hard to run out of this country . . . the mountains. Hard to run, too, knowing what she'd think of him. Hard to run from her.

And he'd taken his two hundred dollars.

It was fight or nothing. Fight, or say goodbye to the Iron, and the county . . . and Catherine.

Say goodbye to Buckskin Frank Leslie, too.

Diller was at the south corral, smearing liniment on a saddle-sore paint. The farrier was a short broad-built man, with a blunt blond head and arms like legs. He had pleasant brown eyes, which were misleading.

"Say, Diller, you get any chance to shoe the pinto?"

"No."

"Needs trimming, too."

"When I get a chance, I'll do it."

Lane had Frank Pace on his mind, and was something less easy than he otherwise might have been.

"Tell you what, now," he said. "When you finish up that bronc, why not trim the pinto and shoe him for me."

"You in a haste?" Diller said.

"Sure am." Though God knew there wasn't pleasure to look forward to in Grover today. Maybe a bullet in the gut, was all.

"Then do your own damn horse's feet—you know where the tools are. I got my own work to do." And back he went, digging in the liniment pot with a stick and smearing the stuff on a back sore as big as a silver dollar.

Lane kicked the farrier hard on the side of the thigh, to charley him.

Diller straightened up with a grunt of pain, and Lane kicked high, catching him in the ribs this time. Diller made a sort of yowling sound, like a cat with a stepped-on tail, and spun to face Lane, already swinging a fist at him. Quick for such a muscled-up fellow, too.

Lane stepped back and drew the Bisley.

"Holy Christ." Diller stared at the revolver like a child at a magic trick, and all the rage went out of him. Lane had seen this before, many times.

Still, there was always something odd and comic about it. A hard, strong fighting man, full of anger as a demijohn of whiskey. Then so suddenly there was the pistol. Like magic. And all the force drained right out of them. You could practically see it going, running down out of them into their boots, out onto the ground.

It had been a pleasure of Lane's, many, many years ago to watch the results of his revolver draw on otherwise brave and violent men. And no shooting necessary, most of the time.

"That is a terrible fast draw you got . . . !" Diller's voice was hoarse with that mingled humiliation and admiration which had, once upon a time, so pleased Lane.

Now it pleased him not at all. He'd kicked an unarmed man, then drawn a pistol on him—showed off a fast draw. A kid's thing to do. A bully's trick.

Would be ashamed, if Catherine Dowd were to see it.

Lane put the Bisley Colt's back in its holster. "I shouldn't have pulled the revolver on you, Diller," he said. "I'm sorry. But I have necessary business in Grover. It won't wait and I need the pinto."

The farrier flushed at this, as though such talk embarrassed him more than gunpoint had. "Hell —I'll get him out and do him for you."

Lane stood by the corral gate and watched Diller work the pinto. He thought, not for the first time, that a gun was a bad thing for a man's manners. Too much, really for a man to have to hold over the head of other men. Of course, Diller took

214

advantage of his strength, where he could; but it wasn't the same thing. There wasn't the threat of death in that.

Lane watched while Diller worked. He offered Diller one of the Grover House cheroots, but the farrier just shook his head and kept on working; ill at ease, Lane supposed, because the disagreement had not ended in a more definite way. In a fight, instead of an apology. People liked things to remain the way they'd always been, even if those ways had been unpleasant. Lane supposed he'd made a worse enemy of Diller than he would have by pistol-whipping him, once he'd gotten the drop.

Diller worked on the pinto's hooves, clipping them with his big trimmers, cutting them down to size, cleaning out the frogs with his hook. Then he'd taken cold shoes from the stack, sized them with some care and nailed them too.

"Done," he said, and let the left fore drop. The pinto, that sturdy horse, had stood the tapping without a twitch. Lane was fond of the pinto.

Lane thanked the farrier, who said nothing to him in return, saddled the horse, tightened the cinch again, and mounted.

He rode the pinto back to the bunk-house, ground-tied him, and went in to get his rifle and boot. Came out and fastened the boot to the saddle-bow, swung up, and rode off down the stable line toward open graze and the Little Chicken a fair ride beyond.

To Grover, by full afternoon.

Lane pulled up in the middle of the horse lot to look back. Grazing mares and their foals lifted

215

their heads to watch him as he sat the pinto. The whole of headquarters was laid out there, held in a shallow green bowl of pine ridge and mountain meadow. He could see the corrals—could almost make out Diller, leading another horse to work. And up to the left, on a slight rise, Charley Drew sitting a long-legged gray with a rifle across his saddle-bow. Charley was watching the head-quarters house.

Lane saw smoke rising from the chimney. The Indian woman would be starting the fire for dinner—lunch, Catherine called it. Making the Dowd's lunch.

Matthew Dowd's, too.

Poor damned little man.

Lane thought it sad the little man had had to pretend with him. Play that he didn't know; didn't know anything. Might have worked for the dollar all the harder, seeing he wasn't making his wife happy. Lane had known a few such.

No pleasure putting horns on any man. Less pleasure nailing them to a midget's forehead. Less honor, too. Any woman but Catherine wouldn't have been worth it.

The pinto cantered along, a short, steady pace that held Lane in a rocking chair saddle. Could dream away, in a pace like that, and let the pinto eat the miles. A plain horse, but the more Lane rode him, the better he liked him. Not much for speed, not like many others, but damn fine for stay. Couldn't ask for a better horse in high mountains, unless it was some fine Appaloosa stallion, and that kind of riding, that kind of living, was years gone past.

The pinto would do and more than do.

Two meadow larks rose up before him as he rode, circled swiftly through the air above him, then climbed and climbed. Lane heard them singing, but when he tilted his Stetson brim and looked up to find them, his vision blurred in the blaze of the sun.

Riding through the high grass, now. Far ahead, over the green-yellow carpet of grass stems—grass-flowers growing among them, red and purple, and all rolling in long soft shallow waves as the wind blew over it—over the grass, Lane saw the line of timber that marked the course of the Little Chicken.

It was a beautiful place, a good place for shade and water. Right about there, he'd made a fool of himself with that bogged cow and calf. Going down in that hole without a dally-rope . . . Some embarrassing, that had been. And, to look back on it, some satisfaction to Dowd, no doubt, seeing Lane make a fool of himself.

Lane reached to·the boot, and pulled the big Sharps up and out. He checked to make sure the piece was loaded—no telling if one of the damn fool drovers might have gone in and messed with it while Lane was out riding—found it so, and let the hammer gently down.

He rode on to the Little Chicken with the rifle across his saddle-bow. Pace might have gotten up early enough to have gotten to the Chicken, be waiting. Not likely, but Lane had known many good men killed by not likely's.

He rode into the trees a half hour later, out of the glare of sunlight, the clouds of insects rising out of the long grass under the pinto's hooves, and into coolness, quiet, and shade.

The Little Chicken ran shallow through the green.

Lane pulled the pinto up at the stream's bank, climbed down, and led the horse down a graveled shelf to drink. The pinto was a time at it, getting its belly full, nuzzling at the clear water, blowing noisily into the ripples.

When he was finished, Lane knelt down and cupped up a drink for himself in his hands.

Sweet water.

He dipped his bandanna into the stream and wiped his face with the wet cloth. Then he led the pinto back up the bank and deeper into the trees. The creek was bringing a cool breeze with its flow. Lane sat beneath a live oak, taking his ease for a little while as the pinto grazed a few yards away, tugging at grass, lipping the tender summer leaves of dwarf willows.

Lane considered some pistol practice, then decided not. If twenty-five years and more of drawing a revolver—and shooting it for effect, more often than not—were not enough practice for him to put Frank Pace down, no few minutes of popping caps would make a difference.

Too damn noisy on such a fine day.

The Chamblee place. Lane hadn't seen it; Clive Chamblee was not the sort of gentleman who invited gunmen to supper. Hadn't seen it, but had heard from the drovers it was prime.

A horse ranch. And not for the first time. There'd been a place years ago, on a river named Rifle.

Not for the first time.

Maybe this one, though . . . This one might stick. Might be a place to stay. Morgan crosses . . .

Lane thought of lighting up a cheroot then decided not. Have to be getting on, getting into town.

He thought of Catherine Dowd for a while. Made a fine ass of himself last night, for sure. Some truth was better not said to a woman. Say you loved them—damn fool!—and sure as hell consequences followed. He'd known that from pimping days. Love: that magic word kept many a fancy-man in silk shirts. Used it himself, and not thought twice about it. It was always a little true, anyway. Any man who could get close up to a fine woman and not feel some love for her, well, not much of a man, there.

That "love" stuff had just popped out. Foolish of him, and unfair to her. Did he really care for her, a gray-headed drifting tramp would have kept his mouth shut and gone on his way.

Was long past this sort of cess, or should be.

Catherine Dowd, for his own and for keeps. An end to wandering, living off his revolver and his knife. An end to making up new names after every trouble . . .

Dream on, jackass! And see what quiet you get, if you do get lucky and kill that Texan. See then if people don't come riding to Grover to see the old rounder killed Frank Pace. See then if a man doesn't call out, "Good Jesus Christ! That's Buckskin Frank Leslie, or I'm a Barbary ape!"

See what quiet you get after that . . .

The revolver gives you a door into death to push other fellows through. All that power over other men. What you pay is, the better you do, the worse you go.

He'd been going bad for years.

Too bad for a lady.

Lane drove into Grover in the afternoon. The streets were some crowded, and Lane saw four drovers he knew, riders for Short-C. Men with no business in town on a workday. A good number of cattlemen in town, he saw. Not looking for trouble; not looking too hard to avoid it, either.

As Lane rode past the feed store, he saw Rex Milford sweeping his loading dock. Milford was an interesting man. More to him, Lane always supposed, than owning a feed store. Something of the gray life about him, still. Tall, thin as a rake, with a big beak of a nose, and pale pop-eyes. A robber, Lane had thought. Might have struck a number of banks, got enough for a stake.

Milford had a habit of glancing over his shoulder when he spoke to you. And Lane had caught him starting to rest his thumb on a gunbelt he no longer wore. An interesting man. He and Lane had occasionally exchanged looks that other men would not have shared.

The crowd was getting thicker. Loafers and

hangers-on, most of them. Two ladybirds from Pott's Parlor standing on the sidewalk, winking and waving at the sports too shy to go up and talk to them. There was a look of hopeful trouble about the people. Lane had seen it many times.

Could be, trouble was coming before him.

He reined the pinto through a group of boys— should have been in Rosie Saunder's school—and turned him alongside the store loading dock.

"Oh-oh," one of the boys behind him said, "here's Dowd's regulator." A boy named Pitcher, a blond small-headed boy with short sense, ran up behind the pinto and near got kicked.

"Say, Mister Lane," he called up, and "Say, Mister Lane!"—The Pitcher boy always said everything twice—"The marshal's goin' to kill that buff from Texas! The Marshal's goin'—"

Lane cut him off. "Is he now, Tom? Why for?"

While the poor halfwit was considering the answer to that, Rex Milford, sweeping up on the planks beside the pinto's head, supplied it. "The Texan beat the marshal, did it last night out back of Mrs. Phelps'." Then he bent back to his sweeping.

Tommy Pitcher, jumping up an down beside Lane's horse, offered the same answer, repeated, but Lane paid no head to him.

"Rough and tumble?" he said to Milford.

"The roughest," the feed store man said, still sweeping, but giving Lane a look. "Say Pace damn near chewed Akins' hand off."

"Right?"

Milford gave Lane another look, somewhat satirical.

"Left."

Well, it was news indeed. Lane rocked back a little in the saddle, thinking about it as Milford swept on down the dock past him, raising a cloud of dust and seed hulls.

"They fit over a gal!" Tommy Pitcher again. "They fit over a gal!"

News indeed. The Porter girl for sure. Akins, considering his tastes, certainly put a value on that girl. Not surprising Pace had beaten him, though. Akins wouldn't have come up against many that caliber in any kind of fight. Still, likely Akins gave the Texan something to think about.

Quite a fight to see, probably, for those who enjoyed watching fist fights. Always seemed something nasty, to Lane, two men hitting each other in the face. God knew he'd done it himself but had never cared for it. Rather would use a knife, if truth were told.

And so, the crowd.

Folks were hoping to see the marshal put the Texan down—as indeed he'd have to if he intended to stay as the law in Grover, the law for all this side of Gunsight Gap.

Not unless he put the Texan down. Or ran him out. Hard to imagine that, not while Pace still had work to do. Would have to try, though, and likely today.

Now . . . now, a smart fellow would climb down off his pinto, tie up right here at the store, and invite Rex Milford over to the Golden Slipper for

222

two or three iced lager beers and a peas and greens and beefsteak dinner. Could sit right over there in the cool out of the heat of afternoon and drink and eat, and listen for the gunshots, the noise of the crowd—*who had seen what, who was down, and how bad hurt* . . .

God knew it would be easy to do. The easiest thing in the world. It was first the law's business, after all, and Akins had already ordered him out of town, ordered him to keep his nose out of trouble in Grover.

Who was he—damn near an old man—to go against a hard-case marshal in his town? And him already posted out.

It was a nacky notion, but it wouldn't do. Akins, already bad hurt, even if not in his gunhand, would have no chance at all against Frank Pace now.

Once he'd killed the marshal, of course, Pace's time in the territory would be coming short. Federal officers from Boise would be riding down soon enough once they'd heard a marshal had been beaten and then shot to death by a hired killer.

Of course, there'd be time enough for Pace to finish what he'd started—to shoot Dowd, or another of the big cattlemen, and a drover or two.

Parris and the sheep people would have their work done.

There was no leaving it all up to Akins—and besides, Lane had taken his two hundred dollars a month. It appeared that he'd surely be earning it.

He took up the pinto's reins again and reached

down with his right hand to touch the butt of the Bisley Colt's. As he did, Lane saw Milford standing up on the dock with his broom in his hand, watching him.

"Good luck," Milford said.

Lane nodded, and touched the pinto with his spurs, cutting away from the store, and out into the middle of the street. The palms of his hands were sweating, and he loosed the reins to wipe them on his trouser legs.

He felt well enough, though. It was odd; he wished in a way that Catherine Dowd was here, in Grover. Just nearby. Foolishness. He should thank God she wasn't.

"Can you kill that Texan? See that you do it, then."

He's as good as dead, Sweetheart—I hope.

Lane rode up the street toward the Grover House. He could see as surely as a ship captain upon the ocean saw the direction of a distant storm that Frank Pace was at the hotel. The faces of dozens of men and women along the streets turned that way as regularly as clock pendulums, interrupting whatever conversations or business or window shopping they were engaged in.

Lane rode up Main Street, wishing he'd put a second pistol into his belt. He hadn't used to want one—wouldn't, in fact, have any chance to use it against a man like Pace. One revolver, one or two shots, and the matter would be decided. Lane had no notion of trying any tricks of sallies against the man, no maneuvers of getting the sunlight into his face, or feints, or firing wild on clearing the holster to shake him for a second, killing shot.

None of that.

He'd see the fellow clear, call him, and kill him if he could.

Two hundred dollars a month. Should have been two thousand.

"Lane!"

At first, Lane didn't know where the call had come from. For an instant he thought it might have been the Texan—then he knew the voice.

He pulled the pinto up, avoiding a buckboard with a crate of chickens in the back, and turned in the saddle to see Harley Akins standing in the doorway of his office. He had a hand on Marcia Porter's shoulder, leaning on her a little, Lane thought, for support.

The marshal was thirty feet away and more, and standing in deep shadow, but Lane saw that Milford had been right. Akins had been badly beaten.

One side of the marshal's face was black with bruising, and he looked to have lost some teeth. His left hand was lost in a wad of white bandage.

Akins took a step out into the sidewalk—took his hand away from the girl's shoulder to do it—and limped as deep as any cripple. He squinted slightly in the sunlight.

"Lane—you were told to stay out of this town." Beaten he might be, but his voice was strong enough. And loud enough. Lane saw two men down the sidewalk turn to listen.

Akins was standing in the sunlight, staring at Lane in his stolid, dangerous, young bull's way. He wore his British pistol in its shoulder holster. Lane wished that Pace had chewed a while on Akins' gun-hand; the boy looked to be making things even tougher than they were.

"I've got business," Lane said. "Won't take long."

"You have got no business at all in this town," Akins said, his voice loud and direct as a travel trunk falling down a flight of stairs.

A little too loud. Lane saw what was happening and saw, too, that there wasn't a damned thing he could do to prevent it. Akins was proving his nerve, and using Lane to do it. Doing this for the watching town but most of all for himself. If it had been just a matter of show, Lane might have passed it off some way. But Harley Akins had something to prove to himself.

Lane tried, anyway.

He edged the pinto nearer the sidewalk. "Listen to me, Marshal," he said. "My business is cattle business; it has nothing to do with you or the law. It is cattle and sheep business. Let us who are paid to settle it, settle it."

Marcia Porter said something from the doorway. Lane couldn't hear it—and Akins put his hand back to stop her saying anything more. "Turn that horse around and clear off," he said to Lane, "or I will arrest you."

Lane saw a horseman pull up down the street. A man and woman came out of a dry goods store to watch.

Time was running short.

Lane kept his voice low. "Let me go on my way, Marshal. If you want, we can settle this matter later."

"We'll settle it now. Get off that mount. You're under arrest." Loud as a trumpet.

Lane lost his temper a little.

"If you're so damned hot for a fight," he said, a little loud himself, "there's a dandy waiting for you up at the hotel!"

Wrong thing to say—and said, likely, because he was feeling nervy himself. Wrong thing to say.

Akins limped off the sidewalk and stepped down into the street. "Harley," the girl said, behind him.

"You bought-and-paid-for dog," Akins said, showing his broken teeth. "Get down from there!" Lane saw him flex the fingers of his gun-hand.

Lane didn't say anything for a moment, keeping hold on himself. *This is not the fight you want . . . not the one you want.*

"I'm riding away from you, Akins. Don't quarrel with me." Damn fool thing to say—it was all he could think of. Lane touched the pinto with his spurs, and the horse moved off at a walk. Lane kept his eyes front. Like a damn cavalry man. No trouble now, boy. Don't cause me more trouble now. He felt Akins' eyes on his back. Easy and easy. Down the street at a walk. That boy back there . . . that damn sissy-boy. Trust the girl . . . Lane heard her saying something.

It was going to be all right. A good distance down the street, now. Lane saw, out of the corner of his eye, the couple standing by the dry goods store. Mister Plaice had put up a display of curtains in his store window, all rigged up as if they were at real windows, with that ruffled thing along the top . . .

"Lane!"

"*Harleee!*"

Lane turned and drew and shot Akins through the hips. The young marshal who had been standing straight, the British pistol held out at arm's length, taking a fine bead, collapsed straight down into the dirt. Marcia Porter jumped off the sidewalk like a boy and ran toward him.

Lane saw the marshal had dropped the heavy pistol when he fell. Now Akins was scrabbling for it, and Lane heard people shouting, and swung the pinto half around—fine horse that hadn't shyed at the shooting—and called to Akins.

"Boy! Boy, don't force me to kill you!"

Akins head was down, not listening. Lane saw him fumble at the big pistol, pick it up. The girl was on him, trying to wrestle for the revolver. She screamed *"Harleee! Harleee!"* like a bird. Akins, half lying in the ruts of the road, raised the pistol and took a good steady rest with his bent elbow. Lane saw the perfect tiny round dot of the muzzle.

He shot the marshal in his face and saw a quick fan of his black hair fly up from behind his head— from the shock, or the bullet's leaving.

Killed him.

Killed the boy.

Marcia Porter stood beside Akins as he stretched out trembling and died. The girl's arms were held up in an odd praying sort of way, but shaking up and down. She was screaming long tearing screams, stopping each time to draw a shuddering breath, then screaming again.

The noise bothered Lane and he turned the horse to ride on down the street. "I've ruined it," he thought. "I've ruined everything."

He spurred the pinto down the street, scattering people in the way. Everyone was staring at him, shouting after him. He saw a horseman down the street pulling away—afraid. He hadn't put the Bisley away—he did it now as he rode. They must think he was running, heading out of town.

They had another thing coming.

He'd played too long with this man from Texas. It was time and past time to kill him. Lane blamed himself for everything. For leaving the Texan alone. For being afraid of him.

And see what happened. '

Everything ruined. Now the Federal Marshal would be coming with his deputies, looking for a man named Lane.

He hauled the running pinto to a sliding stop at the Grover House porch, swung down from the saddle, and saw the Reverend Parris standing inside the hotel at a dining room window, watching him.

Dinner time. Likely Pace would be with him, eating.

Lane left the pinto ground-tied, and walked up the porch steps. Two drummers in checked suits sat in their rockers with their mouths open. Not often a man saw a marshal shot through the head and killed cold. The drummers' faces were white as writing paper.

Lane remembered he had only three loads left in the Bisley. Should have reloaded right after killing Akins. Had never not reloaded after a killing in his life. Getting old and forgetful. Well, three would have to do.

He walked into the lobby, and saw the desk clerk standing up behind the desk. The clerk stared at him, but didn't say anything.

Lane walked across the lobby, his boots silent for a moment on the strip of carpet, then between the two big rubber plants and through the open double doors into the dining room.

This was the finest room in Grover, long and high-ceilinged, painted cream white with gold paint—yellow paint, anyway, edging the ceiling. Long windows down the street side. It was a bright, sunny room, and thirty or forty people were still in it, finishing their dinners.

When Lane came in, he saw that while some people where still eating at the linen covered tables, a lot had gotten up—some with their napkins still tucked into their shirt collars—to go stand at he windows and see what the shooting was about.

The Reverend Parris turned from the first window as Lane walked in, past a waiter, an Indian boy named Jay, standing beside a serving cart. Pieces of cake were lined up on the cart.

Lane was tired of Parris. The man made nothing

but trouble and was in here making more, no doubt.

Parris gave Lane an odd triumphant look, and opened his mouth to say something.

Lane drew and shot him.

Parris, struck in the center of his chest, seemed to slip on the fine waxed floor and fell hard. He lay on the floor between the high window and a table with people still sitting at it, put his hands to his stomach as if the bullet had struck him there, and died.

People flew out of their places like frightened birds and ran shouting away from Lane, running to the windows, running to crouch against the walls, as if he couldn't see them there.

A man at a table in the center of the room didn't get up and run.

He was sitting facing the door, eating a biscuit and watching Lane.

There was a lot of noise in the place. Men shouting. A woman calling to somebody—a child, likely.

The man at the center table finished his biscuit. He kept his eyes on the revolver Lane was holding. When the biscuit was finished, he wiped his lips with his napkin and stood up.

He was half a foot over six feet tall, and had eyes as dark as eyes can get, eyes like a Spanish woman's. His face was bruised; he wore a Remington .44, and a cheap gray suit.

"Say," the man called out to Lane over the noise the people were making—and he turned his head slightly to indicate Parris' corpse, "I owe you one for that." He had a long, sad, serious face. "An awful tiresome fellow."

He had his napkin still held in his left hand; now he put it down on the table in front of him.

People in the room were getting quieter. None of them were moving.

"You'd be Lane, of course," the Texan said.

Lane didn't know why he had not fired at the man the instant he saw and knew him. Something seemed to need to be done and he felt whatever it was coming up in his throat like a cough.

"No," he said. "That's not my name. My name is Frank Leslie. I was called 'Buckskin' sometimes."

Pace stared at him for a long moment, looking thoughtful. Then he said, "That's real bad news." And made the fastest draw that Frank Leslie had ever seen.

The shots rang out together—but wouldn't have; Pace would have had the edge, if Leslie hadn't already had the Bisley in his hand.

The Texan's bullet struck Leslie high in the chest on his right side, and knocked him stumbling back into the serving cart. Leslie fired his second shot as he went—he didn't know if his first had hit Pace at all.

The second struck Frank Pace in the throat.

Leslie shoved the cart out of the way, staggering to stay on his feet, and Pace, his left hand held up to his throat, fired again through a cloud of gunsmoke and hit Leslie along the side of his head and knocked him down.

That shot striking Leslie seemed to make a

terrible breaking noise in his head. It was a sound as if someone had struck his head with a heavy stick, and the stick and his skull had both broken.

"I'm killed," he thought. "This man has killed me."

He believed he was down on the floor, but he couldn't see. He felt the Bisley in his hand, the weight of it. Knew he'd cocked it; had one round left, but couldn't see to shoot. "Oh, help me," he tried to say, and saw odd black revolving wheels. He lifted his head up off the floor—he was right, he had been down—and saw much better at once.

He saw two Frank Paces, one just a bit above the other, grinning at him across a distant table. Blood was squirting from between Pace's clenched teeth, and Leslie saw that Pace was trying to keep the blood in that way.

Both Paces fired at him and Leslie was glad to hear the loud noise of it.

Not killed. Not yet.

He didn't know where Pace's bullet went, but splinters came up from the floor and struck his cheek.

Leslie picked one of the Paces he saw—the lower one, that seemed more solid—and fired his last shot into him.

It seemed to make no difference. Pace stood as straight as ever, looming above his bright red table, blood spurting in quick little jets from between his clenched teeth.

The Remington went slowly up, and Leslie thought he saw the real Pace cock the piece and slowly lower it again to take an aim. Leslie tried to roll away, but he couldn't think of which way to go, and Pace fired at him again.

Leslie felt a sting at his left hand and thought a wasp had gotten into the room. He wished to God he had another round in the Colt's.

Now there was just one Pace, and the Texan did not look displeased. He was smiling a rich red smile. He slowly bowed to Leslie, and fell forward across his red table with a crash, and it rocked and then fell over with him.

Leslie thought he had gone to sleep for a moment, and woke up feeling sick to his stomach. People were running past, not looking down at him, going out of the dining room doors. A woman pulled two children right by him. One of the children, a little boy in a sailor suit, looked down at him as he was pulled past. The little boy's eyes were as round as silver dollars.

Leslie couldn't feel the side of his head—he thought that was where the bullet had gouged him. Might be going to die; he felt sick enough, and he remembered that Pace had shot him somewhere else.

"Oh, dear lord . . . oh, dear lord!"

Leslie heard that and looked up. The desk clerk —the odd-looking one, not the smart young fellow —was leaning over him.

"Are you all right?" the desk clerk said. "Can you get up?"

Leslie thought that was something funny,

feeling as he did. Asking a man shot to pieces if he was all right . . . wanted to get up.

"Hell, yes," he said, and meant that he would like to try to get up. He was surprised to hear himself talk out loud. There was a stink of gunpowder. "Let me try," Leslie said.

The desk clerk put his hands under Leslie's arms and helped him. After he had slipped once and hurt himself, Leslie tried a second time, with the clerk hauling him up. He got to his feet, stood almost straight, and had to bend back over to vomit.

That hurt him badly, but the desk clerk, God bless him, stayed right there with him, holding him up. "God bless you," Leslie said to the man, "for being so kind." Leslie was afraid if he fell again, he'd never get up.

He took a deep breath to try and get some strength, and it made him cough. The right side of his chest hurt when he did that, and he supposed that Pace had touched his lung with that first shot. That was a dangerous thing. That might kill him, right there.

"Do you want to go lie down in the office?" the desk clerk said. "The doctor is coming."

"I'll bleed all over it—I'll mess up your sofa. Just let me stand here and get my breath." There now, that was better. He was feeling worse by the minute, but better about not dying.

"You have a bad wound along the side of your head," the clerk said.

"You think I don't know it? Just be still a

minute and let me stand here."

He remembered he hadn't reloaded the Colt's, and he tried to do it now. It was a lot of work, just trying, and it made Leslie short of breath. He got the gate open, and that was a chore. Then he punched the spent rounds out, and managed to put two fresh loads in. His left hand had blood on the back.

Then he got too sick to do it any more.

"Here, you—sit down!"

Leslie managed to turn his head, and saw a big fat man in a wrinkled suit.

"I don't think I'm going to die, Doc," he said.

"Sit down," Nicholson said. He was regarded in Grover as a strange fellow, but a decent enough medical man, at least for broken bones and such.

"I want to stand," Leslie said. "It hurts to get up. I don't want to go it again."

Nicholson sighed, put his leather satchel on a table, and came and put his fingers on the side of Leslie's head. The desk clerk stood watching, and two other men who Leslie thought had been in the room eating dinner also stood watching, but some distance away. Leslie felt Nicholson pushing and poking there at the side of his head, but it didn't hurt.

While Nicholson was doing that, Leslie tried to see Pace, see where he was down. Surely to God he'd killed the man. At first, he didn't see him. Then he turned his head a little under Nicholson's fingers, and saw Frank Pace lying beside a fallen table. Pace was lying on his side, as if he were asleep, in a wide, spreading pond of blood.

236

Most men, dead, looked smaller. Not Pace.

Nicholson reached into Leslie's shirt—he popped a button off to do it—and put his hand flat against Leslie's chest. That hurt a great deal.

"You have a touched lung there, Mister Lane," the doctor said.

"My name is Buckskin Frank Leslie."

"Now," Nicholson said, "I don't want anymore sauce from you. I want you flat on a bed, and quickly, whatever your name is!"

"I'm persuaded," Leslie said.

And just then, just at the instant he said that, he felt a terrible blow strike him on the back.

It knocked him out of the doctor's hands and hard against the table. He thought he heard a sound at the same time.

Leslie picked the Bisley up off the table, and managed to turn half around.

The little whore Marcia Porter was standing there behind him, over by the door. She had the British revolver held up trembling in both her hands.

Leslie thought of killing her and she saw that and stood still as a rabbit, staring at him through coiling gunsmoke. He thought of killing her, and then thought not. She was a pretty thing.

How Holliday would have laughed. How he would have laughed at this . . .

Leslie felt very tired, and reached out and put the Bisley down on the table. Then he lay down on the floor to rest.

He heard voices, but paid no attention to them. He felt the floor hard against his back. And deep beneath that, he could feel the earth, the whole round earth, slowly, slowly begin to swing away from underneath him. It swung away, like a great door, and left him alone in the dark.

"Catherine . . ." he said.